AMERICAN VOICES FROM

Reconstruction

Reconstruction

Adriane Ruggiero

Marshall Cavendish
Benchmark
New York

Marshall Cavendish Benchmark
99 White Plains Road
Tarrytown, New York 10591-9001
www.marshallcavendish.us

Library of Congress Cataloging-in-Publication Data
Ruggiero, Adriane.
Reconstruction / by Adriane Ruggiero.
p. cm. — (American voices from—)
Summary: "Presents the history of the era of Reconstruction, 1865-1877, through a variety of primary source documents, such as diary entries, newspaper accounts, political speeches, laws, popular songs, and personal letters"—Provided by publisher. Includes bibliographical references and index.
ISBN-13: 978-0-7614-2168-9
ISBN-10: 0-7614-2168-8
1. Reconstruction (U.S. history, 1865–1877)—Juvenile literature. 2. Reconstruction (U.S. history, 1865–1877)—Sources—Juvenile literature. I. Title. II. Series.
E668.R84 2006   973.8'2—dc22
2005024949

Printed in Malaysia
1 3 5 6 4 2

Editor: Joyce Stanton
Editorial Director: Michelle Bisson
Art Director: Anahid Hamparian
Series design and composition: Anne Scatto / PIXEL PRESS

ON THE COVER: A freed slave prepares to vote for the first time (painting by Thomas Waterman Wood, 1868).

ON THE TITLE PAGE: Soldiers roll up their flag after the Confederacy's surrender (painting by Richard Norris Brooke, 1872).

Acknowledgments

The author is grateful to the following organizations for permission to reprint documents:

Frederick Douglass, "What the Black Man Wants," April 1865, in *The Life and Writings of Frederick Douglass,* edited by Philip S. Foner. Reprinted by permission of International Publishers.

Address to the Loyal Citizens and Congress of the United States of America, *Proceedings of the Convention of the Colored People of Virginia, Held in the City of Alexandria, August 2–5, 1865,* Alexandria, VA, 1865. Reprinted with the permission of Simon & Schuster Adult Publishing Group, from *Reconstruction, 1865–1877,* edited by Richard N. Current. Copyright © 1965 by Prentice-Hall, Inc.

Contents

This political cartoon about Northerners settling in to make profits in the South, by Thomas Nast, is a good example of a primary source.

About Primary Sources

What Is a Primary Source?

In the pages that follow, you will be hearing many different "voices" from a special time in America's past. Some of the selections are long, and others are short. You'll find many easy to understand at first reading, while others may require several readings. All the selections have one thing in common, however. They are primary sources. This is the name historians give to the bits and pieces of information that make up the record of human existence. Primary sources are important to us because they are the core material of all historical investigation. You might call them "history" itself.

Primary sources are evidence. They give historians the all-important clues they need to understand the past. Perhaps you have read a detective story in which a sleuth has to solve a mystery by piecing together bits of evidence that he or she uncovers. The detective makes deductions, or educated guesses based on the evidence, and solves the mystery once all the deductions point in a certain direction. Historians work in much the same way.

Thomas Nast, the political cartoonist whose work often appeared in *Harper's Weekly*, greatly influenced public opinion throughout the Civil War and the era of Reconstruction that followed. At right is a little sketch of himself sketching.

Like detectives, they analyze data through careful reading and rereading. After much analysis, they draw conclusions about an event, a person, or an entire era. Different historians may analyze the same evidence and come to different conclusions. That is why there is often strong disagreement about an event.

Primary sources are also called documents. *Documents* is a rather dry word used to describe many different things: an official speech by a government leader, an old map, an act of Congress, a letter worn out from much handling, an entry hastily scrawled in a diary, a detailed newspaper account of an event, a funny or sad song, a colorful poster, a cartoon, a faded photograph, or someone's remembrances captured on tape or film.

By examining the following documents, you the reader will be taking on the role of historian. Here is your chance to immerse yourself in an important period in American history—the era known as Reconstruction, which lasted from the end of the Civil War in 1865 to the withdrawal of the last federal troops from the South in 1877. Through primary sources you will come to know the men and women who lived during that turbulent period. You will hear their points of view in the great debate that took place over how the nation should rebuild and reunite after the devastating war. You will read their often sharply opposing opinions on the meaning of freedom and the role the newly freed slaves should play in society.

How to Read a Primary Source

Each document in this book comes from Reconstruction or the years immediately preceding or following that period. Some documents are from the papers of presidents. Others are selections from laws passed by Congress or state legislatures. There are speeches, letters, and remembrances by politicians, military officers, newspaper editors, teachers, farmers, former slaves, and former slave owners. These documents reflect the opinions of Americans on all sides of the Reconstruction debate, including crusaders who pushed for radical reforms and conservatives who denounced the federal government's actions as "tyranny." All of the documents help us to understand what it was like to live during the Reconstruction era.

As you read each document, ask yourself some basic questions. Who is writing or speaking? Who is that person's intended audience? What is he or she trying to tell the audience? Is the message clearly expressed or is it implied, that is, stated indirectly? What

HARPER'S WEEKLY.

A JOURNAL OF CIVILIZATION.

VOL. XII.—No. 585.]   NEW YORK, SATURDAY, MARCH 14, 1868.   [SINGLE COPIES, TEN CENTS.
[$4.00 PER YEAR IN ADVANCE.

Entered according to Act of Congress, in the Year 1868, by Harper & Brothers, in the Clerk's Office of the District Court of the United States, for the Southern District of New York.

IMPEACHMENT.—THADDEUS STEVENS AND JOHN A. BINGHAM BEFORE THE SENATE.—Sketched by Theodore R. Davis.—[See Page 163.]

Harper's Weekly was an important commentator on Reconstruction. The magazine's articles, editorials, and illustrations have made a huge contribution to our understanding of this period.

words does the writer use to convey his or her message? Are the words emotional or objective in tone? If you are looking at a photograph or drawing, examine it carefully, taking in all the details. What is its content? What is its purpose? How does the photographer or artist reveal his or her feelings about the subject? These are questions that can help you think critically about a primary source.

Some tools have been included with the documents to help you in your investigations. Unusual words have been defined near the selections and in the Glossary at the back of the book. Thought-provoking questions follow each document. These can help focus your reading so that you get the most out of the document. As you read the selections, you will probably come up with many questions of your own. That's great! The work of a historian always leads to many, many questions. Some can be answered, while others will require more investigation. Perhaps when you finish reading this book, your questions will lead you to further explorations of the Reconstruction era.

Soldiers and a former slave make their weary way home after the end of
the Civil War. The artist, Julian Scott, had served in the Union army
and was an eyewitness to scenes like this one.

Introduction

DIVISION AND REUNION

At the end of the Civil War, the South was a conquered, ruined land. The great plantations that had formed the foundation of the Southern agricultural economy were destroyed. Cities, towns, and villages were strewn with the wreckage of war. Millions of former slaves and former slave owners were scattered, with many left homeless and starving. Confederate governments had dissolved. Bandits roamed the land, looting at will. The sole remaining authority was the Union army, whose victorious troops attempted to govern the South and hand out justice in military courts. Meanwhile, federal agents of the newly created Freedmen's Bureau struggled to provide aid and protect the freed slaves.

With their old way of life destroyed and their land occupied, white Southerners felt angry, afraid, and humiliated. For their part, many Northerners were hostile to the defeated Confederate states. They viewed Southerners as traitors and were determined to punish them for seceding, or withdrawing, from the Union and bringing on the devastating war. More moderate voices in the North spoke out for even-tempered justice. The task facing the president was huge: to reunite the country, ensure that the South formed new state governments that were loyal to the Union, and define the role of the freed slaves.

Long before the Civil War ended, Abraham Lincoln had begun to draw up a plan for Reconstruction—the process of reorganizing the seceded states and readmitting them to the Union. Lincoln was a Republican who opposed slavery, but his most important objective was to heal the wounds of war and restore the nation as quickly as possible. His Reconstruction plan called for recognizing new Southern state governments after one-tenth of the state's voters agreed to renounce slavery and took an oath of loyalty to the Union.

Lincoln's moderate plan disturbed a group of Republicans in Congress who favored a more radical restructuring of Southern society. These Radical Republicans were led by two outspoken abolitionists, Thaddeus Stevens in the House of Representatives and Charles Sumner in the Senate. The Radicals called for sweeping changes that would ensure the slave owners never returned to power. They wanted to replace the old plantation system of slaves and masters with a new society based on free labor and equal rights. They also believed that Congress and not the president had the authority for Reconstruction.

President Lincoln was assassinated before he could carry out his Reconstruction plan. His vice president, Andrew Johnson, inherited the difficult task of rebuilding the nation. Johnson was a Democrat who opposed the Radical Republican plan for transforming the South. He quickly instituted a more liberal Reconstruction policy. The new president pardoned thousands of

CONVENTION OF FREEDMEN DISCUSSING THEIR POLITICAL RIGHTS.

former Confederates. He appointed temporary governors to the Southern states and ordered them to organize conventions

Freed slaves hold a meeting in Georgia in 1865, ready to embrace their newly won rights.

where delegates could draw up new state constitutions and form new governments. Johnson's plan set only a few basic requirements for readmission to the Union. Most importantly, the former Confederate states had to renounce secession and agree to the abolition of slavery.

During the first two years of Reconstruction—a period often known as Presidential Reconstruction—the Southern states reestablished their governments under President Johnson's generous plan. Former Confederate leaders dominated the newly elected state legislatures. These lawmakers quickly restored white rule by passing new laws that severely restricted black Americans' rights and freedoms. The "black codes" included vagrancy laws, under which unemployed blacks could be hired out as forced labor, and apprenticing laws, which allowed the courts to take black children from their parents and bind them to the service of white employers. Other laws made it difficult or impossible for blacks to own or rent land, or to work at any job other than agricultural laborer or household servant. Slavery had been abolished, but the former slaves were far from free.

The results of President Johnson's limited approach to Reconstruction outraged the Radical Republicans. Congress refused to recognize the newly formed Southern governments. Demanding greater protection for the rights of the freed slaves, lawmakers passed several bills designed to bring about real and lasting changes in Southern society. These included the Civil Rights Act, which extended citizenship to blacks, and the Reconstruction Acts, which placed the Southern states under military command until the freedmen's rights were guaranteed. Congress also passed the Fourteenth Amendment to the Constitution, defining the basic rights of all citizens, and the Fifteenth Amendment, which gave the vote to all black men. President Johnson opposed all these measures, and the Republican-controlled Congress passed the bills over his veto. Johnson's refusal to compromise on Reconstruction led to increasingly bitter divisions between the president and Congress. In 1868 that conflict reached its climax with the impeachment of the president. Only a single vote prevented Johnson's removal from office.

For the final year of President Johnson's administration and throughout the two terms of his successor, President Ulysses

After the Civil War, African Americans in the South often performed the same work they had done as slaves, such as picking cotton.

Ulysses S. Grant, painted when he was a young army officer

S. Grant, the Radical Republicans played a major role in shaping Reconstruction policy. This period is often called Congressional or Radical Reconstruction. The seceded states were divided into districts, headed by U.S. military commanders. They drew up constitutions that granted black men the vote and restricted former Confederates from voting or holding political office. The newly created Southern governments were dominated by Republicans, including Southern blacks, Northern whites who moved to the South, and Southern white supporters of Radical Reconstruction. The Reconstruction governments restored and modernized the Southern states, rebuilding roads and bridges, constructing new railroads, and reorganizing the court systems. They passed laws prohibiting racial discrimination and protecting the rights of black citizens. One of their greatest achievements was the establishment of public school systems throughout the South.

Despite these accomplishments, most white Southerners

remained bitterly opposed to Reconstruction. During the Grant administration, increasing racial conflicts plagued the South. The anti-Reconstruction Democrats gradually regained control of Southern state governments. Terrorist groups such as the Ku Klux Klan used intimidation and violence to harass blacks and their supporters and to restore white rule. The constant news of race riots, Klan atrocities, government corruption, and election fraud eroded Northerners' support for Reconstruction. Northern political leaders became convinced that the only way to restore peace and stability to the South was to leave Southerners free to manage their own affairs. In 1877 newly elected president Rutherford B. Hayes withdrew the last federal troops from the South, officially ending Reconstruction.

Over the next few decades, a strict policy of segregation, or separation of the races, was established throughout the South. African Americans lost many of the rights they had gained through the Reconstruction reforms. It would be nearly a century before a new generation of civil rights activists resumed the struggle for full freedom and equality and completed the mission begun under Reconstruction.

President Abraham Lincoln, in a portrait made shortly before the beginning of the Civil War.
Lincoln's highest priority was a speedy restoration of the Union.

Chapter I

To Restore the Union

BY THE MIDDLE OF 1863, two years before the end of the Civil War, President Abraham Lincoln was already forming a plan for Reconstruction. The war had started when eleven Southern states withdrew from the Union and formed the Confederate States of America: Alabama, Arkansas, Florida, Georgia, Louisiana, Mississippi, North Carolina, South Carolina, Virginia, Tennessee, and Texas. Lincoln's goal was to restore the seceded states as quickly and easily as possible. He hoped that a policy of forgiveness and generosity would encourage Southerners to form new governments loyal to the Union.

Congressmen from the Radical wing of the Republican Party had other ideas. They supported a stricter approach to Reconstruction, with Congress in charge. The Radical plan aimed to completely revolutionize Southern government and society.

This difference of views would continue after Lincoln's death, leading to harsh conflicts between Congress and Lincoln's successor, Andrew Johnson. Meanwhile, black Americans continued their struggles for equality, arguing that the freedmen would never be truly free until black men were granted the right to vote.

A Traveler Describes the Devastated South

After the Civil War the South lay in poverty and ruins. A Northerner who traveled through Alabama's Tennessee River Valley described the plight of plantation owners and the newly freed slaves.

"I have seen more than one great plantation absolutely deserted."

THE TRAIL OF WAR IS VISIBLE throughout the valley in burnt-up gin-houses, ruined bridges, mills, and factories, and in large tracts of once cultivated lands stripped of every vestige [trace] of fencing. . . . The roads, long neglected, are in disorder, and having in many places become impassable, new tracks have been made through the woods and fields without much respect to boundaries. Borne down by losses, debts, and accumulating taxes, many who were once the richest among their fellows have disappeared from the scene, and few have yet risen to take their places. . . . When the war ended, and the bond of slavery was dissolved, . . . swarms [of freedmen] went off to seek new masters in the field of free labour, and after a season of trials, often bitter, are only returning by degrees to their old homes. . . . I have seen more than one great plantation absolutely deserted, . . . void of fence or labour.

—*From Robert Somers,* The Southern States Since the War 1870–1.
New York: Macmillan, 1871.

The Civil War left many parts of the South, such as this section of Charleston, South Carolina, in ruins.

THINK ABOUT THIS

1. What signs of the war's impact did the writer observe?
2. Why do you think the freedmen returned to the plantations?

President Lincoln Offers the Ten-Percent Plan

In December 1863 Abraham Lincoln offered a plan of "restoration" to the Southern people. The president's Proclamation of Amnesty and Reconstruction embodied what came to be known as the Ten-Percent Plan. After at least 10 percent of a seceded state's voters took an oath to support the Constitution and the Union, the state could legally establish a new government. Lincoln's proclamation assumed that the authority for Reconstruction belonged to the president, and it offered a full pardon, or amnesty, for former Confederates who took the loyalty oath.

WHEREAS, IN AND BY the Constitution of the United States, it is provided that the President "shall have power to grant reprieves and pardons for offences against the United States, except in cases of impeachment"; and

Whereas, a rebellion now exists whereby the loyal state governments of several states have for a long time been subverted, and many persons have committed, and are now guilty of, treason against the United States; . . .

Therefore, I, Abraham Lincoln, President of the United States, do proclaim . . . to all persons who have, directly or by implication, participated in the existing rebellion . . . that a full pardon is hereby granted to them . . . with restoration of all rights of property, except as to slaves . . . upon the condition that every such person shall take and subscribe an oath . . . :

"I, ———, do solemnly swear, in presence of Almighty God, that I will henceforth faithfully support, protect, and defend the Constitution of the United States and the Union of the States thereunder; and that I will, in like manner, abide by and faithfully support all acts of Congress passed during the existing rebellion with reference to slaves. . . ."

The persons excepted from the benefits of the foregoing provisions are all who are, or shall have been, civil or diplomatic officers or agents of the so-called Confederate government; . . . all who are, or shall have been, military or naval officers of said so-called Confed-

" . . . a full pardon is hereby granted them . . . with restoration of all rights of property, except as to slaves."

erate government above the rank of colonel in the army or of lieu-
tenant in the navy; [and] all who left seats in the United States Congress to aid the rebellion. . . .

And I do further proclaim, declare, and make known that whenever,
in any of the States of Arkansas, Texas, Louisiana, Mississippi, Tennessee, Alabama, Georgia, Florida, South Carolina, and North Carolina, a number of persons, not less than one tenth in number of the
votes cast in such state at the presidential election of the year of our
Lord [1860], each having taken the oath, . . . shall re-establish a
state government . . . , such [government] shall be recognized as the
true government of the state.

—*From Abraham Lincoln's Proclamation of Amnesty and Reconstruction,
December 8, 1863. Available online at www.history.umd.edu/Freedmen/procamn.htm*

THINK ABOUT THIS

1. What are the three key provisions of the loyalty oath?
2. What types of people are excluded from Lincoln's pardon? Why do you think he chose to exclude those groups?

Radical Republicans Propose a Stricter Policy

Two leaders of the Radical Republicans, Senator Benjamin Wade
and Representative Henry Winter Davis, answered Lincoln's Ten-
Percent Plan with a much stricter proposal. The Wade-Davis Bill
placed the authority for Reconstruction with Congress. It required
that at least 50 percent of a seceded state's voters take the loyalty
oath before the state could reestablish its government. The bill also
included harsh punishments for former Confederates, including

the restrictions outlined in the sections below. Congress passed the Wade-Davis Bill in 1864, but President Lincoln refused to sign it into law.

usurpation
seizure of power

SECTION 4. . . . No person who has held or exercised any office, civil or military, state or confederate, under the rebel usurpation, or who has voluntarily borne arms against the United States, shall . . . be eligible to be elected as delegate [to a constitutional convention]. . . .

SECTION 7. . . . The convention shall declare, on behalf of the people of the state, their submission to the constitution and laws of the United States, and shall adopt the following provisions, . . . and incorporate them in the constitution of the state, that is to say:

First. No person who has held or exercised any office, civil or military, . . . under the usurping power, shall vote for or be a member of the legislature, or governor.

Second. Involuntary servitude is forever prohibited, and the freedom of all persons is guaranteed. . . .

Senator Benjamin Wade, one of the leaders of the Radical Republicans, urged strict conditions upon which Southern states could be readmitted to the Union.

SECTION 14. . . . . Every person who shall hereafter hold or exercise any office, civil or military, . . . in the rebel service, state or confederate, is hereby declared not to be a citizen of the United States.

—From the Wade-Davis Bill, July 8, 1864. In Henry Steele Commager, editor, Documents of American History, 6th edition. New York: Appleton-Century-Crofts, 1958.

THINK ABOUT THIS

1. What types of people does the bill punish? What are the forms of punishment?

2. Do you think the punishments are fair and reasonable?

Congress Passes the Thirteenth Amendment

The Emancipation Proclamation, issued by President Lincoln in January 1863, abolished slavery in all states "in rebellion against the United States." A few months later, Republican senators proposed a constitutional amendment to expand emancipation and make sure it would continue after the war's end. Congress approved the Thirteenth Amendment in January 1865 and sent it to the states for ratification. Under President Lincoln's Reconstruction plan, Southern legislatures were required to approve the amendment before their states could return to the Union. The Civil War ended in April 1865 and in December of that year the Thirteenth Amendment became part of the Constitution, making slavery forever illegal throughout the United States.

With the passage of the Thirteenth Amendment, auction houses like this one—photographed in Atlanta, Georgia, in the early 1860s—would finally disappear from the American landscape.

"Neither slavery nor involuntary servitude . . . shall exist within the United States."

SECTION 1. Neither slavery nor involuntary servitude, except as a punishment for crime whereof the party shall have been duly convicted, shall exist within the United States, or any place subject to their jurisdiction.

SECTION 2. Congress shall have power to enforce this article by appropriate legislation.

—From the Thirteenth Amendment to the U.S. Constitution (1865). Available online at http://caselaw.lp.findlaw.com/data/constitution/amendment13

1. Some historians have called the Thirteenth Amendment the most important measure of the nineteenth century. Do you agree?
2. In Section 1, is it significant that the United States is referred to in the plural?
3. A proposed amendment must be ratified by three-fourths of the states in order to become part of the Constitution. Why do you think the framers of the Constitution made the amendment process so difficult?

Lincoln Promises "Charity for All"

Abraham Lincoln was sworn in for a second term as president in March 1865. Thousands of people gathered in the shadow of the newly completed Capitol dome in Washington, DC, to hear Lincoln's second inaugural address. In this brief, powerful speech, the president anticipated the war's end in little more than a month and reached out to all Americans.

FELLOW-COUNTRYMEN: . . . On the occasion corresponding to this four years ago all thoughts were anxiously directed to an impending civil war. All dreaded it, all sought to avert it. While the inaugural address was being delivered from this place, devoted altogether to saving the Union without war, urgent agents were in the city seeking to destroy it without war—seeking to dissolve the Union and divide [its] effects by negotiation. Both parties deprecated war, but one of them would make war rather than let the nation survive, and the other would accept war rather than let it perish, and the war came.

    One-eighth of the whole population were colored slaves, not distributed generally over the Union, but localized in the southern

deprecated
strongly disapproved of

Lincoln himself wrote the famous "malice toward none" speech that he delivered at his second inauguration.

the sword, as was said ~~three~~ thousand years ago, so still it must be said "the judgments of the Lord, are true and righteous altogether"

With malice toward none; with charity for all; with firmness in the right, as God gives us to see the right, let us strive on to finish the work we are in; to bind up the nation's wounds; to care for him who shall have borne the battle, and for his widow, and his orphan— to do all which may achieve and cherish a just and a lasting peace, among ourselves, and with all nations,

part of it. These slaves constituted a peculiar and powerful interest. All knew that this interest was somehow the cause of the war. To strengthen, perpetuate, and extend this interest was the object for which the insurgents would rend the Union even by war, while the Government claimed no right to do more than to restrict the territorial enlargement of it. Neither party expected for the war the magnitude or the duration which it has already attained. Neither anticipated that the cause of the conflict might cease with or even before the conflict itself should cease. Each looked for an easier triumph, and a result less fundamental and astounding. . . . Fondly do we hope, fervently do we pray, that this mighty scourge of war may speedily pass away. . . .

With malice toward none, with charity for all, with firmness in the right as God gives us to see the right, let us strive on to finish the work we are in, to bind up the nation's wounds, to care for him who shall have borne the battle and for his widow and his orphan, to do all which may achieve and cherish a just and lasting peace among ourselves and with all nations.

"...let us strive on to finish the work we are in, to bind up the nation's wounds."

—*From Abraham Lincoln's Second Inaugural Address, March 4, 1865.*
Available online at http://www.bartleby.com/124/pres32.html

THINK ABOUT THIS

1. Who do you think is Lincoln's intended audience—Northerners, Southerners, or both?
2. How does the speech reflect his views on Reconstruction?

Frederick Douglass Explains "What the Black Man Wants"

Frederick Douglass was a leading spokesperson for African-American rights before, during, and after the Civil War. Douglass had been born a slave. He escaped to freedom as a young man, and gained fame as an abolitionist lecturer, writer, and newspaper publisher. In this speech to the Massachusetts Anti-Slavery Society, delivered a few days before the war's end, he explained the significance of voting rights for the freed slaves.

enfranchisement
the act of giving someone the right to vote

I HAVE HAD BUT ONE IDEA for the last three years to present to the American people. . . . I am for the "immediate, unconditional and universal" enfranchisement of the black man, in every State in the Union. Without this, his liberty is a mockery; without this, you might as well almost retain the old name of slavery for his condition; for in fact, if he is not the slave of the individual master, he is the slave of society, and holds his liberty as a privilege, not as a right. He is at the mercy of the mob, and has no means of protecting himself. . . .

We want [the vote] because it is our right, first of all. No class of men can, without insulting their own nature, be content with any deprivation of their rights. We want it, again, as a means for educating our race. Men . . . derive their conviction of their own possibilities largely by the estimate formed of them by others. If nothing is expected of a people, that people will find it difficult to contradict that expectation. . . .

There are, however, other reasons, not derived from any consideration merely of our rights, but arising out of the conditions of the South. . . . I believe that when the tall heads of this Rebellion shall have been swept down, . . . there will be this rank undergrowth of

Frederick Douglass dedicated his life to obtaining freedom and full civil rights for African Americans.

treason . . . interfering with, and thwarting the quiet operation of the Federal Government in those states. . . . Now, where will you find the strength to counterbalance this spirit, if you do not find it in the Negroes of the South? . . . I hold that the American people are bound, not only in self-defence, to extend this right to the freedmen of the South, but they are bound by their love of country, and by all their regard for the future safety of those Southern States, to do this— to do it as a measure essential to the preservation of peace there.

"I am for the 'immediate, unconditional and universal' enfranchisement of the black man."

—From Frederick Douglass, *"What the Black Man Wants,"* April 1865. Available online at http://www.frederickdouglass.org/speeches/#wants

THINK ABOUT THIS

1. What do you think Douglass means by the metaphorical expression, "this rank undergrowth of treason"?
2. Do you agree with his statement that people need to have expectations placed on them?
3. What arguments does Douglass use to support his demand for black enfranchisement?

A Freedmen's Convention Appeals to Congress

As the Civil War drew to a close, and after it was over, former slaves joined together in conventions to discuss ways to safeguard their hard-won liberty. One meeting held in Alexandria, Virginia, in

August 1865, drew thousands of freedmen as well as abolitionists. After four days of speeches and discussions, the delegates to the convention issued the following appeal to Congress.

WE, THE UNDERSIGNED MEMBERS of a Convention of colored citizens of the State of Virginia, would respectfully represent that, although we have been held as slaves, and . . . deprived of the dearest rights of human nature: yet when you and our immediate oppressors met in deadly conflict upon the field of battle . . . *we*, with scarce an exception, in our inmost souls espoused your cause. . . .

espoused
supported

When the contest waxed long, and the result hung doubtfully, you appealed to us for help, and how well we answered is written in the rosters of the two hundred thousand colored troops now enrolled in your service. . . .

Well, the war is over, the rebellion is "put down" and we are *declared* free! Four-fifths of our enemies are paroled or amnestied, and the other fifth are being pardoned, and the

Two of the many African Americans who fought as soldiers in the Union army, captured on film by the famous Civil War photographer Matthew Brady

President has, in his efforts at the reconstruction of the civil government of the States, . . . left us entirely at the mercy of these subjugated but unconverted rebels. . . . We *know* these men—know them *well*—and we assure you that, with the majority of them, loyalty is only "lip deep," and that their professions of loyalty are used as a cover to the cherished design of getting restored to their former relations with the Federal Government, and then, by all sorts of "unfriendly legislation," to render the freedom you have given us more intolerable than the slavery they intended for us. . . .

In one word, the only salvation for us besides the power of the Government is in the *possession of the ballot.* Give us this, and we will protect ourselves. . . .

We are "sheep in the midst of wolves," and nothing but the military arm of the Government prevents us and all the *truly* loyal white men from being driven from the land of our birth. Do not then, we beseech you, give to one of these "wayward sisters" the rights they abandoned and forfeited when they rebelled until you have secured *our* rights by [an] amendment to the Constitution.

"We are 'sheep in the midst of wolves.'"

—From *"Address to the Loyal Citizens and Congress of the United States of America,"*
Proceedings of the Convention of the Colored People of Virginia,
Held in the City of Alexandria, August 2–5, 1865, *Alexandria, VA, 1865.*
Reprinted in Richard N. Current, editor, Reconstruction, 1865–1877.
Englewood Cliffs, NJ: Prentice-Hall, 1965.

THINK ABOUT THIS

1. What do the freedmen fear?
2. What important argument do they use to demonstrate their loyalty?
3. How do you think they expect voting rights to protect them from "unconverted rebels"?

President Johnson Reviews His Policies

On April 14, 1865, Abraham Lincoln was shot and fatally wounded at Ford's Theatre in Washington, DC. Following his death, Andrew Johnson was sworn in as president. Johnson was a former Democratic senator from Tennessee who had remained loyal to the Union during the Civil War, earning him the Republican nomination for vice president in the election of 1864. The new president was also a former slave owner who believed that "white men alone must manage the South." Under his moderate Reconstruction plan, provisional, or temporary, governors were appointed to the Southern states and ordered to call constitutional conventions, where white Southern representatives could draft state constitutions. The newly established state governments were required to renounce secession and ratify the Thirteenth Amendment, abolishing slavery. No other measures protecting the rights of the freed slaves were required. By the end of

Andrew Johnson was a former slaveholder and had little interest in guaranteeing the rights of African Americans. Matthew Brady made this photograph not long after Johnson was sworn in as president.

1865, Johnson had recognized the new governments of nearly all of the former Confederate states. In his year-end address to Congress, he reviewed his actions during his early months as president.

PROVISIONAL GOVERNORS have been appointed for the States, conventions called, governors elected, legislatures assembled, and Senators and Representatives chosen to the Congress of the United States. . . .

The next step which I have taken to restore the constitutional relations of the States has been an invitation to them to participate in the high office of amending the Constitution. . . . On the one side the plan of restoration shall proceed in conformity with a willingness to cast the disorders of the past into oblivion, and . . . on the other the evidence of sincerity in the future maintenance of the Union shall be put beyond any doubt by the ratification of the proposed amendment to the Constitution, which provides for the abolition of slavery forever within the limits of our country. . . .

". . . the plan of restoration shall proceed in conformity with a willingness to cast the disorders of the past into oblivion."

Every danger of conflict is avoided when the settlement of the question [of black suffrage] is referred to the several States. They can, each for itself, decide on the measure, and whether it is to be adopted at once and absolutely or introduced gradually and with conditions. In my judgment the freedmen, if they show patience and manly virtues, will sooner obtain a participation in the elective franchise through the States than through the General Government, even if it had power to intervene. When the tumult of emotions that have been raised by the suddenness of the social change shall have subsided, it may prove that they will receive the kindest usage from some of those on whom they have heretofore most closely depended.

—From Andrew Johnson's First Annual Message to Congress, December 4, 1865. In James D. Richardson, editor, A Compilation of the Messages and Papers of the Presidents, *volume VI. Washington, DC: U.S. Government Printing Office, 1897.*

THINK ABOUT THIS

1. How does Johnson's speech reveal his most important concerns in dealing with the former Confederate states?
2. What is his policy regarding black voting rights? How do you think the freedmen reacted to his statements on this issue?

The Black Codes Restrict Freedmen's Rights

The Southern state governments established under President Johnson's Reconstruction plan were dominated by former Confederate leaders. Southern legislatures quickly passed a series of laws to restore white control over the newly freed slaves. These "black codes" sharply limited the freedmen's rights and freedoms and helped ensure that blacks would continue to serve as laborers for white employers. Following are selections from laws passed by the Mississippi state legislature in November 1865.

CIVIL RIGHTS OF FREEDMEN IN MISSISSIPPI

SECTION 6. All contracts for labor made with freedmen, free Negroes, and mulattoes . . . shall be in writing . . . ; and if the laborer shall quit the service of the employer before the expiration of his term of service, without good cause, he shall forfeit his wages for that year.

"Every civil officer shall . . . arrest and carry back to his or her legal employer any freedman, free negro, or mulatto who shall have quit . . . without good cause."

SECTION 7. . . . Every civil officer shall, and every person may, arrest and carry back to his or her legal employer any freedman, free negro, or mulatto who shall have quit the service of his or her employer before the expiration of his or her term of service without good cause. . . .

mulattoes
people of mixed black and white ancestry

MISSISSIPPI APPRENTICE LAW

SECTION 1. . . . It shall be the duty of all sheriffs, justices of the peace, and other civil officers . . . to report . . . all freedmen, free negroes, and mulattoes, under the age of eighteen, . . . who are orphans, or whose parent or parents have not the means or who refuse to provide for and support said minors; and thereupon it shall be the duty of [the] court to apprentice said minors to some competent and suitable person, on such terms as the court may direct. . . .

SECTION 3. . . . In the management and control of said apprentice, said master or mistress shall have the power to inflict such moderate

corporeal chastisement
physical punishment

corporeal chastisement as a father or guardian is allowed to inflict on his or her child. . . .

SECTION 4. . . . If any apprentice shall leave the employment of his or her master or mistress, without his or her consent, said master or mistress may pursue and recapture said apprentice. . . .

Under the black codes, the situation for many freed slaves was scarcely better than it had been before emancipation.

MISSISSIPPI VAGRANCY LAW

SECTION 2. . . . All freedmen, free negroes, and mulattoes in this State, over the age of eighteen years, found . . . with no lawful employment or business, or found unlawfully assembling themselves together either in the day or nighttime, . . . shall be deemed vagrants, and, on conviction thereof shall be fined . . . and imprisoned.

—*From "The Black Codes of Mississippi 1865." In Henry Steele Commager, editor,* Documents of American History, *6th edition. New York: Appleton-Century-Crofts, 1958.*

THINK ABOUT THIS

1. In what ways did Mississippi's laws violate the civil rights of black Americans?
2. How did the black codes benefit white employers?

Chapter 2

The Freedmen's Bureau

ONE MONTH BEFORE the end of the Civil War, Congress established the Bureau of Refugees, Freedmen, and Abandoned Lands, commonly known as the Freedmen's Bureau. The Freedmen's Bureau was a temporary agency, set up to operate for one year under the administration of the War Department. At its peak of operations, it had only nine hundred agents. Nevertheless, the bureau had a vital mission: to provide aid and services to the hundreds of thousands of Southerners who had been left poor and homeless by the Civil War.

Freedmen's Bureau officials provided food, clothing, and medical care to needy Southerners, both black and white. In the summer of 1865, they distributed 150,000 daily food rations, with one-third going to white refugees. Over time, however, most of the bureau's services benefited the freed slaves. Those special services included helping black communities establish churches and schools, supervising labor relations between former slaves and former masters, and protecting the freedmen from mistreatment and violence.

Children, like these huddling in the ruins of Charleston,
were among the many refugees who needed the assistance of the
Freedmen's Bureau after the Civil War.

At first the Freedmen's Bureau had no trouble raising funds to fulfill its many duties. Congress gave the new agency the authority to take over all lands and property abandoned by plantation owners fleeing the advancing Union troops. Some of the confiscated lands were sold to finance bureau operations, while other plots were rented to freedmen, often in return for a share of their crops. All across the South, landless black families were thrilled by rumors that the government intended to give every former slave "forty acres and a mule." In early 1866 those hopes were dashed when President Johnson returned all confiscated lands to their pre–Civil War owners. Johnson's actions not only shattered the freedmen's dreams of land ownership but also eliminated the main source of funding for the Freedmen's Bureau.

Congress voted twice to extend the life of the Freedmen's Bureau. In January 1869 most bureau operations were discontinued, and in 1872, the agency was completely terminated. Lack of funding and opposition from conservatives in both the North and the South had prevented bureau officials from accomplishing many of their ambitious goals. Despite these obstacles, however, the Freedmen's Bureau did help thousands of African Americans achieve rights they had been denied during slavery.

Congress Establishes the Freedmen's Bureau

The Freedmen's Bureau was the first federal agency to provide social welfare to Americans. Congress passed the act establishing the bureau on March 3, 1865. The Freedmen's Bureau Act detailed the new agency's three-part mission: to provide social services to freed slaves and white refugees, to take control of Confederate lands that had been seized by the Union Army, and to parcel out the confiscated lands to the freedmen. Here is a portion of the act.

BE IT ENACTED by the Senate and House of Representatives of the United States of America in Congress assembled, That there is hereby established in the War Department, to continue during the present war of rebellion, and for one year thereafter, a bureau of refugees, freedmen, and abandoned lands, to which shall be committed . . . the supervision and management of all abandoned lands, and the control of all subjects relating to refugees and freedmen from rebel states. . . . The said bureau shall be under the management and control of a commissioner to be appointed by the President, by and with the advice and consent of the Senate. . . .

SECTION 2. . . . The Secretary of War may direct such issues of provisions, clothing, and fuel, as he may deem needful for the immediate and temporary shelter and supply of destitute and suffering refugees and freedmen and their wives and children. . . .

SECTION 4. . . . The commissioner, under the direction of the President, shall have authority to set apart, for the use of loyal refugees and freedmen, such tracts of land within the insurrectionary states as shall have been abandoned, or to which the United States shall have acquired title by confiscation or sale, or otherwise, and to every male citizen, whether refugee or freedman . . .

". . . to every male citizen, whether refugee or freedman . . . there shall be assigned not more than forty acres."

there shall be assigned not more than forty acres of such land, and the person to whom it was so assigned shall be protected in the use and enjoyment of the land for the term of three years. . . . At the end of said term, or at any time during said term, the occupants of any parcels so assigned may purchase the land.

—From "An Act to Establish a Bureau for the Relief of Freedmen and Refugees," March 3, 1865. Available online at http://www.history.umd.edu/Freedmen/fbact.htm

THINK ABOUT THIS

1. What could freedmen and refugees expect to receive from the Freedmen's Bureau?
2. Why do you think land ownership was so important to the freed slaves?

An Official Finds "Confusion" in North Carolina

Union army general Oliver Otis Howard was appointed commissioner of the Freedmen's Bureau, and assistant commissioners were assigned to each of the Southern states. Colonel E. Whittlesey was assistant commissioner for North Carolina. In this report he describes the conditions he found on his arrival in the state capital, Raleigh.

ON THE 22D OF JUNE I ARRIVED at Raleigh with instructions . . . to take control of all subjects relating to "refugees, freedmen, and the abandoned lands" within this State. I found these subjects in much

As commissioner of the Freedmen's Bureau, General Oliver Otis Howard was responsible for seeing that former slaves received the services they needed to begin their new lives as free citizens.

confusion. Hundreds of white refugees and thousands of blacks were collected about this and other towns, occupying every hovel and shanty, living upon government [food] rations, without employment and without comfort, many dying for want of proper food and medical supplies. A much larger number, both white and black, were crowding into the towns, and literally swarming about every depot of supplies to receive their rations. . . .

The street in front of the post's commissary's office was blocked up with vehicles of all the descriptions peculiar to North Carolina, and with people who had come from the country around . . . for government rations. These were destitute whites, and were supplied by order of the department commander. Our own headquarters, and every office of the bureau, was besieged from morning till night by freedmen, some coming many miles on foot, others in wagons and carts. The rations issued would scarcely last till they reached home. . . .

I have made every effort to protect them [the freedmen] from wrong. Suddenly set free, they were at first exhilarated by the air of liberty, and committed some excesses. To be sure of their freedom, many thought they must leave the old scenes of oppression and seek new homes. Others regarded the property accumulated by their labor as in part their own, and demanded a share of it. On the other hand, the former masters, suddenly stripped of their wealth, at first looked upon the freedmen with a mixture of hate and fear. In these circumstances some collisions were inevitable. The negroes were complained of as idle, insolent, and dishonest; while they complained that they were treated more cruelly than when they were slaves. . . . All officers of the bureau were directed . . . to investigate these difficulties between the two classes, to settle them . . . as far as possible, to punish light offences by fines or otherwise, and to report more serious cases of crime to the military authorities for trial.

—From "Freedmen's Bureau Report, North Carolina, 1865" in Report of the Joint Committee on Reconstruction of the First Session Thirty-Ninth Congress. Washington, DC: U.S. Government Printing Office, 1866.

THINK ABOUT THIS

1. According to the commissioner, what were the most pressing problems in Raleigh?
2. What beliefs and attitudes caused conflicts between former masters and former slaves?

A Tennessee Official Reports on Violence against Blacks

Many Southern whites, embittered by losses suffered during and after the war, lashed out at the former slaves. The Freedmen's Bureau was charged with investigating and punishing all such violent attacks. In this letter a bureau official expresses his frustration about the "outrages" committed in his district in Tennessee.

JANUARY 15, 1866 . . .

Since April 15 [1865] there have been numerous outrages committed against freedmen in this district. The violence committed was generally death. . . . During the rebellion the freedman was kept under the control of their rebel master by violence for if any left their former master they sent the young bands of Bushwhackers after him and when [he] was found he was deliberately shot down. This deterred many from leaving and this today keeps them from getting remuneration for their work. . . .

Bushwhackers
Confederate guerrillas

There is still lingering in this county a set of desperadoes that have never yet submitted to the civil authorities, armed to the hilt, who are still the terror to the freedmen, urged up no doubt by the citizens here. It so happened that a freedman had done some work for a bar keeper in Vernon in this county for which he applied for a settlement and while in the house 3 of them outlaws entered and commenced up on the Black man, all to abuse him, first with words. The freedman made no resistance and started to leave whereupon they drew their side arms and deliberately presented at his

"There is . . . a set of desperadoes . . . armed to the hilt, who are still the terror to the freedmen."

As this cartoon from 1875 shows, soldiers stationed in the South were needed to protect African Americans from violence for many years after the end of the Civil War. Note the sign in the background for the KKK.

head. Fortunately it failed fire, whereupon [an outlaw] seized a butcher knife and ran after him, the Negro being the strongest seized him and threw him to the ground and held him until some one interfered and made a settlement of the difficulty as all through. But he was no sooner released when [another man] gathered an axe and made after him again, this time the Negro ran some 2 or three hundred yards and kept out of the way. . . . When he got him back [they] commenced the 3rd time with bricks and rocks, succeeded in striking him several times, bruising him up severely. I attempted to have this matter thoroughly investigated but could get nobody or persons to arrest the parties. I even tried the Military who also refuse. . . .

There is every disposition that can be conceived of to thwart the workings of the Bureau. If anything is wrong on the part of the freedman I must do something and when I attempt to right it every conceivable obstacle is thrown in my way. . . .

M. H. Puckett . . .
Hickman County Tenn.

—From "Report of Outrages, Riots and Murders, Jan. 15, 1866–Aug. 12, 1868," National Archives Microfilm Publication M999, Roll 34. Available online at http://freedmensbureau.com/tennessee/reports/centreville.htm

1. What does the official believe is behind the attacks on the freedmen?
2. What problems does he face in trying to do his job?

The Case of "Freedman Dan"

One important area of Freedmen's Bureau operations involved family services. The agency provided information and assistance to unite the families of former slaves and helped relocate hundreds of thousands of people left stranded by the war. In this letter, a bureau officer in South Carolina arranges transportation for a freedman left all alone in Charleston.

[August 1866]
Lt. Col. H. W. Smith . . .
Charleston, S.C.

Colonel,
    I have the honor to request that transportation may be furnished for the destitute freedman Dan from this place to Newberry, S.C. He was brought here by his owners some two years ago to prevent his falling into the hands of our forces and has been left here by them. He is almost blind and can do no work. His connections live at Newberry and have sent for him to go to them, they promising to provide for him. There will in all probability be a scarcity of provisions here next year and unless

"He was brought here by his owners . . . and has been left here by them."

this man can be sent to his family he must become a charge to this Bureau. . . .

your Obedt. [Obedient] Servant
William Stone

—From "Records of the Assistant Commissioner for the State of South Carolina," National Archives Publication M869, Roll 44. Available online at http://www.freedmensbureau.com/southcarolina/transportation/transportation5.htm

THINK ABOUT THIS

1. How did Dan become stranded in South Carolina?

2. How do you think his relatives might have learned his location?

Nine-Year-Old Harriet Norwood Is Apprenticed

Former slave owners often tried to trick former slaves into working for them under terms that were little different from the old slavery system. The Freedmen's Bureau protected these workers by drawing up fair labor contracts that spelled out the terms of employment, including work responsibilities, wages, and benefits such as lodging, food, clothing, and medical care. Bureau officials also drew up agreements of indenture, or apprenticeship, for orphans and children whose parents could not provide for them. These contracts bound a child to work for an employer for a specified period of time in return for food, lodging, and instruction in a trade. In the following indenture agreement, Freedmen's Bureau

Household chores made up the bulk of African-American women's work both before and after the Civil War.

official Fred W. Thibaut acts as guardian for nine-year-old Harriet Norwood in her apprenticeship to William G. John.

TO ALL WHOM IT MAY CONCERN
Greeting:

This indenture made and entered into on this tenth day of October in the year of our Lord One Thousand Eight Hundred and Sixty Seven at Washington in the County of Hempstead in the state of Arkansas by and between Fred W. Thibaut . . . , Superintendent of Freedmen's, Refugees, etc, and . . . guardian of one Harriet Norwood, a freed girl, an orphan minor having no estate for her maintenance and education, aged nine years, and William G. John. . . .

· · ·

The said Fred W. Thibaut . . . does hereby put, place and bind out the said Harriet Norwood . . . to the said William G. John to learn the art of housekeeping, cooking, washing, ironing and sewing from the date hereof until Harriet Norwood shall arrive at the age of eighteen years—during all of which time the said Harriet Norwood shall well and faithfully serve the said William G. John, and everywhere and at all times obey his lawful commands. . . . She shall not contract matrimony during the period for which she is hereby apprenticed without the knowledge and consent of said John. She shall not absent herself from the service of said John; but shall in all things and at all times behave and conduct herself as a good and faithful apprentice ought to do. . . .

> *"She shall . . . at all times behave and conduct herself as a good and faithful apprentice ought to do."*

And the said William G. John on his part does hereby covenant, promise and agree, to teach and instruct the said Harriet Norwood . . . in the art or business of housekeeping, cooking, washing, ironing and sewing; to well and faithfully provide for the said apprentice sufficient meat, drink, clothing, lodging and all other necessaries. . . .

And the said William G. John does hereby further covenant and bind himself to teach said apprentice or cause her to be taught reading, writing, and arithmetic.

—From "Indentures of Apprenticeship Dec. 1865–Feb. 1868, Contracts: Jan. 1, 1865–Jan. 1, 1868," National Archives Microfilm Publication M999, Roll 20. Available online at http://freedmensbureau.com

THINK ABOUT THIS

1. What are the benefits to both parties in this apprenticeship arrangement?
2. Who do you think benefits most?

A Northern Teacher Founds
a Freedmen's School

Under the slave laws it was illegal to teach a slave to read and write. When the first schools for freed slaves opened after the Civil War, they were crowded to overflowing with eager students, adults and children alike. Most freedmen's schools were founded and operated by Northern charitable associations or by Southern black men and women who had been secretly educated. The Freedmen's Bureau helped by supervising the new schools, renting buildings for classrooms, contributing funds for books and other supplies, paying for the transportation of teachers, and providing military protection for students and teachers against white Southerners who violently opposed black education. In the following letter, teacher Edmonia Highgate describes her encounters with eager students and hostile townspeople in

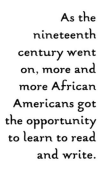

As the nineteenth century went on, more and more African Americans got the opportunity to learn to read and write.

Louisiana. The daughter of freed slaves living in New York, High-gate had traveled south near the war's end to establish freedmen's schools on behalf of a Christian charity.

December 17th, 1866

Dear Friend:

Perhaps you may care to know of my work here for the Freed people. . . . I have a very interesting and constantly growing day school, a night school, and, a glorious Sabbath School of near one hundred scholars. The school is under the auspices of the Freedman's Bureau, yet it is wholly self-supporting. The majority of my pupils come from plantations, three, four and even eight miles distant. So anxious are they to learn that they walk these distances so early in the morning as never to be tardy. Every scholar buys his own book and [writing] slate, etc. . . . They, with but few exceptions are french Creoles. My little knowledge of French is just [enough] to instruct them in our language. They do learn rapidly. A class who did not understand any English came to school last Monday morning and at the close of the week they were reading "Easy Lessons." . . . Most of the men, women and large children are hired by the year "on contract" upon the plantations of their former so called masters. One of the articles of agreement is that the planter shall pay "a five percent tax for the education of the children of his laborers." . . .

There is more than work for two teachers yet I am all alone, God has wonderously spared me. There has been much opposition to the School. Twice I have been shot at in my room. Some of my night-school scholars have been shot but none killed. A week ago an aged freedman was shot so badly as to break his arm and leg—just across the way. The rebels here threatened to burn down the school and

French Creoles
persons of mixed French and black descent

"The rebels here threatened to burn down the school."

house in which I board before the first month was passed. Yet they have not materially harmed us. The nearest military Jurisdiction is two hundred miles distant at New Orleans. . . .

Yours for Christ's poor,
Edmonia G. Highgate

—From Amistad Research Center, American Missionary Association Archives, Tulane University, New Orleans, Louisiana. Available online at http://www.pbs.org/wgbh/amex/reconstruction/schools/ps_highgate.html

THINK ABOUT THIS

1. What were some of the challenges Highgate faced as a teacher in a freedmen's school?

2. What hardships did the students endure to get an education?

A Southerner Advises, "Leave the People to Themselves"

White Southerners resented the "interference" of the federal agents of the Freedmen's Bureau. Testifying before a congressional committee investigating conditions in the South, magazine editor James D. B. DeBow of New Orleans expressed a widely held point of view: if the North would just leave them alone, Southerners could easily work out their problems.

QUESTION: What is your opinion of the necessity or utility of the Freedmen's Bureau? . . .

ANSWER: I think if the whole regulation of the negroes, or freedmen, were left to the people of the communities in which they live, it will be administered for the best interest of the negroes as well as of the white men. I think there is a kindly feeling on the part of the planters towards the freedmen. They are not held at all responsible for anything that has happened. They are looked upon as the innocent cause. In talking with a number of planters, I remember some of them telling me they were succeeding very well with their freedmen, having got a preacher to preach to them and a teacher to teach to them, believing it was for the interest of the planter to make the negro feel reconciled; for, to lose his services as a laborer for even a few months would be very disastrous. . . . Leave the people to themselves, and they will manage very well. The Freedmen's Bureau, or any agency to interfere between the freedman and his former master, is only productive of mischief.

—*From the testimony of James D. B. DeBow before the Joint Committee on Reconstruction, March 28, 1866, in* Report of the Joint Committee on Reconstruction of the First Session Thirty-Ninth Congress. *Washington, DC: U.S. Government Printing Office, 1866.*

THINK ABOUT THIS

1. What does DeBow's testimony reveal about his attitude toward blacks?
2. What argument does he use to explain why former masters would, if left to their own devices, treat the freedmen fairly?
3. How do you think a former slave might have responded to his comments?

A Cartoonist Honors the Freedmen's Bureau

During the Reconstruction period, *Harper's Weekly* was America's leading magazine of social and political commentary. The magazine's news columns, strongly worded editorials, and political cartoons gave it a distinctive voice that both reflected and helped shape public opinion. *Harper's Weekly* was a strong supporter of Radical

Reconstruction and the Freedmen's Bureau. This cartoon, by Alfred R. Waud, appeared in the July 25, 1868 issue, just as the bureau was being closed down. It was meant to honor the organization's three years of work. The figure in the center represents the bureau.

Among its other accomplishments, the Freedmen's Bureau prevented many violent confrontations between former slaves and former slaveholders.

THINK ABOUT THIS

What do you think the cartoonist is saying about the role of the Freedmen's Bureau?

Chapter 3

Congress versus the President

UNDER PRESIDENT Andrew Johnson's Reconstruction plan, thousands of former Confederate leaders regained control of Southern state governments. Southern legislatures quickly passed the discriminatory black codes and elected former Confederates to the U.S. Senate. Even moderate Republicans worried that Johnson's policies seemed to be rewarding old enemies and restoring rebel governments, while Radicals denounced the president's actions as "madness."

Congress took its first steps to oppose Presidential Reconstruction in December 1865. Returning from a long recess, the lawmakers refused to recognize the new Southern state governments or admit their newly elected senators. Then they began to draft a series of proposed laws designed to protect the freed slaves. One by one the president vetoed the bills. One by one Congress passed them over his veto. Johnson's stubborn refusal to compromise on Reconstruction gradually pushed many conservative and moderate Republicans into the Radical camp. For his part, the president denounced Congress's actions and

President Johnson hindered enforcement of Reconstruction legislation to such an extent that Congress eventually impeached him. This 1868 illustration shows Johnson, seated, listening to the opening speech at his impeachment trial.

did everything in his power to prevent enforcement of the anti-discrimination laws.

In 1868 the increasingly bitter struggle between the president and Congress resulted in Johnson's impeachment. While the president's opponents were unsuccessful in their attempt to remove him from office, they succeeded in stripping him of power. For the remainder of Johnson's administration, control over the Reconstruction process would pass from the president to Congress.

Thaddeus Stevens Advocates Social Revolution

In December 1865 Republican lawmakers returned from recess determined to unravel President Johnson's Reconstruction policies. A committee of fifteen senators and representatives was formed to develop an alternate congressional plan. One of the most outspoken members of the Joint Committee

Thaddeus Stevens urged a radical reorganization of the South, including its "manners," "habits," "institutions"—and property.

on Reconstruction was Thaddeus Stevens, a representative from Pennsylvania and a leader of the Radical Republicans. Stevens believed that the Southern states should not be readmitted to the Union until they gave the freedmen land and the vote. In this speech delivered in his hometown of Lancaster, the crusading lawmaker advocated strict federal control of the South, with the aim of revolutionizing its society and institutions.

THE ARMIES OF THE CONFEDERATE STATES having been conquered and subdued, and their territory possessed by the United States, it becomes necessary to establish governments therein which shall be republican in form and principles and form a more "perfect Union" with the parent government. It is desirable that such a course should be pursued as to exclude from those governments every vestige of human bondage, and render the same impossible in this nation. . . .

We hold it to be the duty of government to inflict condign punishment on the rebel belligerents, and so weaken their hands that they can never again endanger the Union; and so reform their municipal institutions as to make them republican in spirit as well as in name.

condign
appropriate

We especially insist that the property of the chief rebels should be seized. . . .

There are about six millions of freedmen in the South. . . . By thus [confiscating] the estates of the leading rebels, the government would have 394,000,000 of acres. . . . Divide this land into convenient farms. Give, if you please, forty acres to each adult male freedman. . . .

"The whole fabric of southern society must be changed."

This plan would, no doubt, work a radical reorganization in Southern institutions, habits and manners. It is intended to revolutionize their principles and feelings. . . . The whole fabric of southern society must be changed, and never can it be done if this opportunity is lost. . . .

If the South is ever to be made a safe Republic, let her lands be cultivated by the toil of the owners, or the free labor of intelligent citizens. This must be done even though it drive her nobility into exile. If they go, all the better. . . . It is far easier and more beneficial to exile 70,000 proud, bloated and defiant rebels, than to expatriate four millions of laborers, native to the soil and loyal to the Government.

expatriate
banish

—*From Thaddeus Stevens's speech in Lancaster, Pennsylvania, September 6, 1865. Available online at http://www.anselm.edu/academic/history/hdubrulle/CivWar/text/documents/doc50.htm*

THINK ABOUT THIS

1. What words convey Stevens's feelings about the former Confederates?
2. Do you think the freed slaves were entitled to the land of former plantation owners?

The Civil Rights Act Combats the Black Codes

The Civil Rights Act of 1866 was the first major piece of Radical Republican legislation. The law counteracted the discriminatory black codes by extending the rights of citizenship to all black Americans, whether they had been born slave or free. In one sense this was a dramatic break with the past. In 1857 the Supreme Court had ruled in the controversial Dred Scott case that slaves could *not* be considered citizens. At the same time the law was considered a moderate measure, since it did not give blacks the vote or allow them to sit on juries.

BE IT ENACTED, That all persons born in the United States and not subject to any foreign power, excluding Indians not taxed, are hereby declared to be citizens of the United States; and such citizens, of every race and color, without regard to any previous condition of slavery or involuntary servitude, except as punishment for crime whereof the party shall have been duly convicted, shall have the same right, in every State and Territory in the United States, to make and enforce contracts, to sue, be parties [to lawsuits], and give evidence, to inherit, purchase, lease, sell, hold, and convey real and personal property, and to full and equal benefit of all laws and proceedings for the security of person and property, as is enjoyed by white citizens, and shall be subject to like punishment, pains, and penalties, and to none other, any law, statute, ordinance, regulation, or custom to the contrary.

". . . citizens, of every race and color, . . . shall have the same right . . . to full and equal benefit of all laws."

—From the Civil Rights Act of 1866. In Henry Steele Commager, editor, Documents of American History, *6th edition. New York: Appleton-Century-Crofts, 1958.*

THINK ABOUT THIS

1. How does the Civil Rights Act define the basic rights of all American citizens?
2. How does it take the authority to grant citizenship away from the states and give it to the federal government alone?

Harper's Weekly Asks, "Why Not Call Them Citizens?"

Congress passed the Civil Rights Bill on March 13, 1866. Two weeks later, President Johnson vetoed it, declaring that the newly freed slaves were not ready for the privileges and responsibilities of citizenship. Johnson also argued that the legislation was unconstitutional because it interfered with the rights of state governments. *Harper's Weekly* responded with this editorial defending the federal government's authority to establish the citizenship of the freedmen. On April 9 the Civil Rights Bill became law when Congress passed it over the president's veto.

THE CIVIL RIGHTS BILL was drawn with simplicity and care for a very necessary purpose. It declares who are citizens of the United States, defines their rights, prescribes penalties for violating them, and provides means of redress [righting a wrong]. . . .

It is certainly essential . . . that the true meaning of citizenship should be defined. Nearly a fifth of the population of the country are colored. . . . They are native to the soil. They owe and perform the obligations of other citizens. Why not call them citizens? . . .

The Dred Scott decision declared that a free negro was not a citizen. In 1862, under the Government purged of the influence of slavery, the question again arose, and [the government] . . . held that color was not a disqualification. But the baffled party of disunion [the Democrats] still asserts the contrary. President Johnson in his veto of the Civil Rights Bill admits a difference of opinion; and the Constitution, while it speaks of citizens, nowhere defines the term. It is therefore both timely and wise, at the close of a civil war which has abolished slavery, that the highest authority should declare distinctly who are citizens of the United States, and what are the rights to which citizens are entitled.

The policy of such a measure is plain from the fact that the civil rights of millions of the native population of the United States are destroyed in certain parts of the country on the ground of color; that this invasion springs from the spirit and habit of slavery, and that, if not corrected by the supreme authority, the inevitable result will be a confirmation of that spirit, and a consequent perpetual menace of the public peace. . . . Nothing can tend so surely to confirm the peace of the Union as the kindly but firmly expressed intention of the Government to protect and enforce the equal civil rights of every citizen.

"It is therefore both timely and wise . . . that the highest authority should declare distinctly who are citizens of the United States."

—From *"The Civil Rights Bill,"* Harper's Weekly, *April 14, 1866. Available online at http://blackhistory.harpweek.com/4Reconstruction/226TheCivilRightsBill.htm*

THINK ABOUT THIS

1. Why does the writer believe that it is necessary to define the "true meaning of citizenship"?
2. What does he believe would be the result of *not* defining citizenship?

The Fourteenth Amendment Protects Civil Rights

Republicans were afraid that the Civil Rights Act did not go far enough to protect the rights and security of the freed slaves. Even before the bill was passed, the Joint Committee on Reconstruction began working on a constitutional amendment that would prevent former Confederates from returning to power and guarantee basic civil rights to all citizens, black and white. The amendment also was meant to encourage Southern states to grant black suffrage, by reducing congressional representation for states that did not give black men the vote. Congress passed the Fourteenth Amendment on June 13, 1866. Following are the first three sections of the amendment.

SECTION 1. All persons born or naturalized in the United States, and subject to the jurisdiction [authority] thereof, are citizens of the United States and of the state wherein they reside. No state shall make or enforce any law which shall abridge [limit] the privileges or immunities [protections] of citizens of the United States; nor shall any state deprive any person of life, liberty, or property, without due process of law; nor deny to any person within its jurisdiction the equal protection of the laws.

". . . nor shall any state deprive any person of life, liberty, or property, without due process of law."

SECTION 2. Representatives shall be apportioned among the several states according to their respective numbers, counting the whole number of persons in each state, excluding Indians not taxed. But when the right to vote at any election . . . is denied to any of the male inhabitants of such state [who are] citizens of the United States, . . . the basis of representation therein shall be reduced. . . .

SECTION 3. No person shall be a Senator or Representative in Congress . . . or hold any office, civil or military, under the United States, or under any state, who . . . shall have engaged in insurrection or rebellion against the same.

—*From Amendment XIV to the U.S. Constitution. Available online at http://www.law.cornell.edu/constitution/constitution.amendmentxiv.html*

THINK ABOUT THIS

1. What actions does the amendment prohibit states from taking?

2. The writers of the amendment hoped that future lawmakers would be able to broaden its protections. Which phrases in section 1 do you think were left deliberately vague in order to allow later interpretations?

Congress Places the South under Military Rule

Ten of the Southern state governments established under President Johnson's Reconstruction plan refused to ratify the Fourteenth Amendment. (The only exception was Tennessee, which approved the amendment and was readmitted to the Union in July 1866.) In response, Congress passed a bill abolishing the existing Southern governments and placing the South under military rule. The legislation, called the First Reconstruction Act, required the seceded states to adopt new constitutions ratifying the Fourteenth Amendment and granting voting rights to black men. On March 2, 1867, President Johnson vetoed the

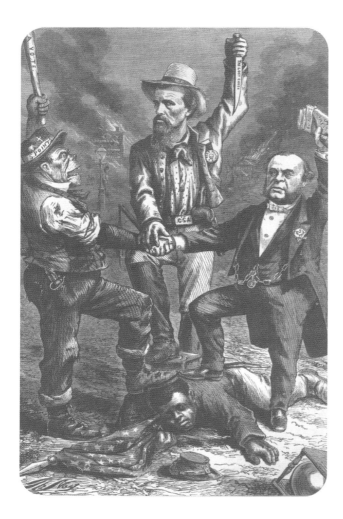

A Thomas Nast political cartoon from 1868, commenting on the Democratic Party's determination to trample the newly won rights of African Americans

bill. That same day both houses of Congress passed it over his veto. Three additional Reconstruction Acts were passed in 1867 and 1868, spelling out the complete details of Congressional Reconstruction. Here are portions of the First Reconstruction Act.

BE IT ENACTED, That [the] rebel States shall be divided into military districts and made subject to the military authority of the United States. . . .

SECTION 2. That it shall be the duty of the President to assign to the command of each of said districts an officer of the army . . . and to detail a sufficient military force to enable such officer to perform his duties and enforce his authority. . . .

SECTION 3. That it shall be the duty of each officer assigned as aforesaid, to protect all persons in their rights of person and property, to suppress insurrection, disorder, and violence, and to punish, or cause to be punished, all disturbers of the public peace. . . .

SECTION 5. That when the people of any one of said rebel States shall have formed a constitution of government in conformity with the Constitution of the United States in all respects, framed by a convention of delegates elected by the male citizens of said State, twenty-one years old and upward, of whatever race, color, or previous condition, . . . except such as may be dis[en]franchised for participation in the rebellion or for felony at common law, and when such constitution shall provide that the elective franchise shall be enjoyed by all . . . persons . . . , and when said State . . . shall have adopted the [Fourteenth] amendment to the Constitution of the United States, . . . said State shall be declared entitled to representation in Congress. . . .

". . . it shall be the duty of each officer . . . to suppress insurrection, disorder, and violence."

SECTION 6. That, until the people of said rebel States shall be by law admitted to representation in the Congress of the United States, any civil governments which may exist therein shall be deemed provisional [temporary] only, and in all respects subject to the paramount authority of the United States.

—From George P. Sanger, editor, The Statutes at Large: Treaties and Proclamations of the United States of America from December 1865 to March 1867, *volume 14. Boston: Little, Brown, 1868.*

THINK ABOUT THIS

1. What were the responsibilities of the military governors of the five Southern districts?

2. How could Southern states regain their representation in Congress?

President Johnson Opposes the Reconstruction Acts

In a December 1867 message to Congress, President Johnson explained his opposition to the Reconstruction Acts and called for their repeal. One of his chief arguments was that the acts would establish governments dominated by the freedmen, who he believed were incapable of carrying out the rights and responsibilities of leadership.

IT IS MANIFESTLY AND AVOWEDLY the object of these laws to confer upon negroes the privilege of voting and to dis[en]franchise such a number of white citizens as will give . . . [black voters] a clear majority at all elections in the Southern States. . . .

"It is manifestly and avowedly the object of these laws to confer upon negroes the privilege of voting."

It is not proposed merely that they shall govern themselves, but that they shall rule the white race, make and administer State laws, elect Presidents and members of Congress, and shape . . . the future destiny of the whole country. Would such a trust and power be safe in such hands? . . .

The plan of putting the Southern States wholly and the General Government partially into the hands of negroes is proposed at a time peculiarly unpropitious. The foundations of society have been broken up by civil war. Industry must be reorganized, justice reestablished, . . . and order brought out of confusion. To accomplish these ends would require all the wisdom and virtue of the great men who formed our institutions originally. I confidently believe that their descendants will be equal to the arduous task

President Johnson, defending his policies, addresses a crowd gathered outside the White House.

before them, but it is worse than madness to expect that negroes will perform it for us.

—From President Johnson's Third Annual Message to Congress, December 3, 1867. In James D. Richardson, editor, A Compilation of the Messages and Papers of the Presidents, volume VI. Washington, DC: U.S. Government Printing Office, 1897.

THINK ABOUT THIS

How would you respond to President Johnson's argument that it was dangerous to give inexperienced black voters a lot of power?

Congress Impeaches the President

President Johnson could not prevent Congress from passing the Reconstruction Acts, but he could use the power of his office to weaken their impact. One of the ways the president defied Congress was by dismissing government officials who were serious about enforcing the laws. His actions outraged Radical Republicans and turned many former supporters against him. In early 1868 the power struggle reached a climax. After Johnson dismissed Secretary of War Edwin Stanton, a supporter of Congressional Reconstruction, the House voted to impeach the president. In the impeachment process,

Johnson's impeachment trial dragged on for more than two months.

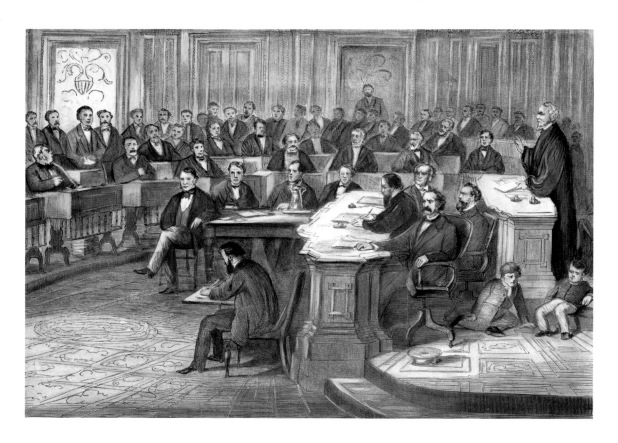

the House of Representatives charges a president with "high crimes and misdemeanors," and the Senate must determine whether he is guilty of the charges and therefore should be removed from office. The first eight of the eleven charges against Johnson dealt with his violation of the Tenure of Office Act, which prohibited the president from dismissing federal officials without Senate approval.

". . . Andrew Johnson, President of the United States, . . . did attempt to bring into disgrace . . . the Congress of the United States."

ARTICLE I. That said Andrew Johnson, President of the United States, . . . unmindful of the high duties of his office, of his oath of office, and of the requirement of the Constitution that he should take care that the laws be faithfully executed, did unlawfully and in violation of the Constitution and laws of the United States issue an order in writing for the removal of Edwin M. Stanton from the office of Secretary for the Department of War . . . with intent then and there to violate the act entitled "An act regulating the tenure of certain civil offices". . . .

ARTICLE X. That said Andrew Johnson, President of the United States, unmindful of the high duties of his office and the dignity and proprieties thereof, and of the harmony and courtesies which ought to exist and be maintained between the executive and legislative branches of the Government of the United States, . . . did attempt to bring into disgrace, ridicule, hatred, contempt, and reproach the Congress of the United States . . . and to excite the odium and resentment of all the good people of the United States against Congress and the laws [that] it duly and constitutionally enacted [and did] make and deliver with a loud voice certain intemperate, inflammatory, and scandalous harangues, and did therein utter loud threats and bitter menaces, as well against Congress as the laws of the United States.

—From "Proceedings of the Senate Sitting for the Trial of Andrew Johnson, President of the United States, in Articles of Impeachment exhibited by the House of Representatives." In Henry Steele Commager, editor, Documents of American History, 6th edition. New York: Appleton-Century-Crofts, 1958. Also available online at http://www.law.umkc.edu/faculty/projects/ftrials/impeach/articles.html

THINK ABOUT THIS

1. Which article makes it clear that the real reason for Johnson's impeachment was his opposition to Congress?

2. What words and phrases reflect the strong emotions behind the Republicans' attempt to remove Johnson from office?

Senator Sumner Calls for Johnson's Removal

Andrew Johnson's impeachment trial began on March 4, 1868. A number of senators argued for convicting the president, including Radical Republican leader Charles Sumner, whose speech is excerpted below. Other senators spoke out in Johnson's defense. Even some Republicans who personally opposed Johnson's policies worried that removing him from office would weaken the executive branch, encouraging future lawmakers to impeach any president who disagreed with them. On May 16 the Senate voted on the final article of impeachment, which charged that the pres-

This caricature of Radical Republican leader Charles Sumner was drawn four years after Johnson's impeachment trial.

ident's dismissal of Stanton was "a high misdemeanor in office." Thirty-five senators found Johnson guilty—just one vote short of the two-thirds necessary to convict him. After a second vote taken ten days later yielded the same result, the president was cleared of all charges.

THIS IS ONE OF THE last great battles with slavery. Driven from these legislative chambers, driven from the field of war, this monstrous power has found a refuge in the Executive Mansion, where, in utter disregard of the Constitution and laws, it seeks to exercise its ancient, far-reaching sway. . . .

Slavery has been our worst enemy, assailing all, murdering our children, filling our homes with mourning, and darkening the land with tragedy; and now it rears its crest anew, with Andrew Johnson as its representative. . . .

He took to himself legislative powers in the reconstruction of the Rebel states; and, . . . in vindication of this misconduct, uttered

The official tally of the Senate's vote on Johnson's impeachment

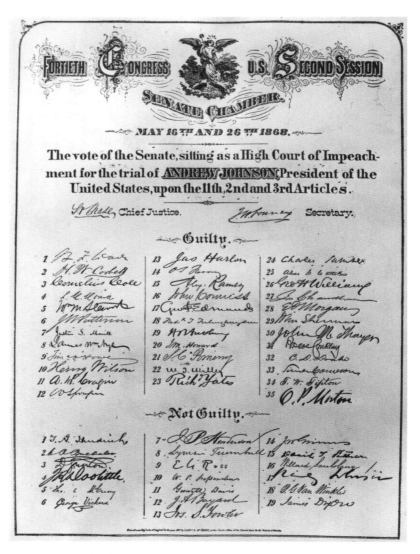

a scandalous speech in which he openly charged members of Congress with being assassins, and mentioned some by name. . . .

More than one person was appointed provisional governor who could not take the oath of office required by act of Congress. . . . The effect of these appointments was disastrous. They were in the nature of notice to Rebels everywhere, that participation in the rebellion was no bar to office. . . . And thus all offices from governor to constable were handed over to a disloyal scramble. . . .

The powers of the Senate over appointments were trifled with and disregarded by reappointing persons who had been already rejected. . . . The veto power conferred by the Constitution as a remedy for ill-considered legislation was turned by him into a weapon of offense against Congress. . . . The power of removal, which Patriot presidents had exercised so sparingly, was seized as an engine of tyranny and openly employed to maintain his wicked purposes. . . .

Laws enacted by Congress for the benefit of the colored race . . . were first attacked by his veto; and when finally passed by the requisite majority over his veto, were treated by him as little better than dead letters. . . .

For all these, or any one of them, Andrew Johnson should have been impeached and expelled from office.

—From "Charles Sumner, Opinion on the Trial of Andrew Johnson, 1868." In Brenda Stalcup, editor, Reconstruction. San Diego, CA: Greenhaven Press, 1995. Also available online at http://odur.let.rug.nl/~usa/D/1851–1875/reconstruction/ch_sumner.htm

THINK ABOUT THIS

1. Are Sumner's arguments based more on facts or emotions? What words and phrases back up your answer?
2. Do you find his arguments convincing? Why or why not?

The Fifteenth Amendment Gives Black Men the Vote

While the Reconstruction Acts required Southern states to grant black suffrage, black men still could not vote in most Northern states. In February 1869 Congress addressed that injustice by proposing a constitutional amendment. The Fifteenth Amendment

Fortieth Congress of the United States of America;

At the *third* Session,

Begun and held at the city of Washington, on Monday, the *seventh* day of *December*, one thousand eight hundred and sixty-eight.

A RESOLUTION

Proposing an amendment to the Constitution of the United States.

Resolved by the Senate and House of Representatives of the United States of America in Congress assembled, (two-thirds of both Houses concurring) That the following article be proposed to the legislatures of the several States as an amendment to the Constitution of the United States, which, when ratified by three-fourths of said legislatures shall be valid as part of the Constitution, namely:

Article XV.

Section 1. The right of citizens of the United States to vote shall not be denied or abridged by the United States or by any State on account of race, color, or previous condition of servitude —

Section 2. The Congress shall have power to enforce this article by appropriate legislation —

Schuyler Colfax
Speaker of the House of Representatives

B. F. Wade
President of the Senate pro tempore.

Attest:
Edw. McPherson
Clerk of House of Representatives.

Geo. C. Gorham
Secy of Senate U.S.

An original draft proposal of the Fifteenth Amendment

would forbid any state to deny male citizens the right to vote on the grounds of "race, color, or previous condition of servitude." All Southern states that had not yet been reconstructed were required to approve the amendment before they could rejoin the Union. The amendment was ratified in February 1870.

SECTION 1. The right of citizens of the United States to vote shall not be denied or abridged by the United States or by any state on account of race, color, or previous condition of servitude.

SECTION 2. The Congress shall have power to enforce this article by appropriate legislation.

—From Amendment XV to the U.S. Constitution. Available online at http://www.law.cornell.edu/constitution/constitution.amendmentxv.html

THINK ABOUT THIS

1. Radical Republicans proposed a form of the Fifteenth Amendment that forbade states to impose additional conditions for voting, such as literacy tests or property ownership requirements. Do you think those extra protections should have been added?

2. Why do you think moderates might have opposed the stronger version of the amendment?

New railroads, in addition to improved roads, bridges,
and public buildings, were signs of economic progress in the South
under the Radical Republicans.

The Radicals Take Charge

ALTHOUGH ANDREW JOHNSON was cleared of the charges brought against him in his impeachment trial, the controversy had left him with little remaining power or influence. In 1868 the Republicans nominated General Ulysses S. Grant for president. The popular Civil War hero easily won the election. During his two terms in office, Radicals dominated the Republican Party and shaped Reconstruction policy.

By 1870, all of the Southern states had been readmitted to the Union under the terms of the Reconstruction Acts. The new state governments were dominated by the pro-Reconstruction Republican Party. These governments were comprised mainly of three groups: black Southerners; white Northerners who had moved to the South to seek political office, known as "carpetbaggers"; and Southern white supporters of Reconstruction, known as "scalawags" by their opponents.

The mission of the Reconstruction governments was to restore the Southern economy and protect the freedmen's rights. Southern legislatures directed the rebuilding of roads, bridges, and public buildings and voted funds for the construction of new railroads. They passed laws designed to ensure that blacks could participate as full citizens in Southern economic and political life. They also established statewide public school systems, offering millions of children of both races their first chance for a free education.

Despite these accomplishments, the majority of white Southerners bitterly resented being governed by Northerners and former slaves. Claiming that the new governments were incompetent and corrupt, these opponents worked to restore white rule and overthrow the Reconstruction governments.

A Black Congressman Defends His Right to Hold Office

On average, about 15 to 20 percent of the officeholders in Reconstruction governments were black. To supporters of Reconstruction, the image of black men governing states that until recently had held them in bondage was an inspiring sign of social progress. To opponents, it was an outrage. In 1868 Democrats in the Georgia legislature attempted to expel black members, claiming that they were unfit to serve. Among the black congressmen was Henry McNeal Turner. Turner had been born to free black parents in Columbia, South Carolina. After the war he moved to Georgia, helped organize the state's Republican Party, and won election to the state House of Representatives. In the following speech to the Georgia legislature, he defended the right of blacks to hold political office and warned of dire consequences if that right was

denied. Despite his impassioned appeal, Georgia Democrats succeeded in expelling fifteen black congressmen. Two years later, however, the federal government forced Georgia to readmit its black legislators.

Hiram Revels was the nation's first African-American senator. This French engraving shows his swearing-in ceremony in 1870.

I HOLD THAT I AM A member of this body. . . . I shall neither fawn nor cringe before any party, nor stoop to beg them for my rights. . . . I am here to demand my rights, and to hurl thunderbolts at the men who would dare to cross the threshold of my manhood. . . .

[Black men] have pioneered civilization here; we have built up your country; we have worked in your fields, and garnered your harvests, for two hundred and fifty years! And what do we ask of you in return? . . . We ask you, now, for our *rights*. . . .

You may expel us, gentlemen, but I firmly believe that you will someday repent it. The black man cannot protect a country, if the country doesn't protect him; and if, tomorrow, a war should arise, I would not raise a musket to defend a country where my manhood is denied. . . .

Where have you ever heard of four millions of freemen being governed by laws, and yet have no hand in their making? . . . How dare you to make laws by which to try me and my wife and children, and deny me a voice in the making of these laws? . . .

You may think you are doing yourselves honor by expelling us from this House; but when we go, we will . . . light a torch of truth that will never be extinguished. . . . When you expel us, you make us forever your political foes, and you will never find a black man to vote a Democratic ticket again.

"You may expel us, gentlemen, but I firmly believe that you will someday repent it."

—*From Henry McNeal Turner's speech to the Georgia Legislature, September 3, 1868. In Edwin S. Redkey, editor,* Respect Black: The Writings and Speeches of Henry McNeal Turner. *New York: Arno Press, 1971.*

THINK ABOUT THIS

1. How does Turner justify his demand for the right of black men to hold political office?
2. What does he say will happen if that right is denied?

A Northerner Becomes a "Carpetbagger"

A number of Northerners moved south after the Civil War to take part in the region's political reorganization. These Northern white officeholders became a significant force in Southern state governments, holding about one-third of all government posts. Resentful white Southerners gave the unwelcome visitors a scornful nickname: carpetbagger. The term came from the name for a common type of traveler's bag made of carpet material. According to Southern critics, the carpetbaggers were lowly crooks who came to rob the state treasuries, carrying all their worldly possessions in a carpetbag. In reality, most carpetbaggers were Freedmen's Bureau officials, former Union soldiers, teachers, clergymen, or businessmen. In this narrative a Northern immigrant to South Carolina explains how he came to be known as a carpetbagger. He also mentions the term *scalawags*—the belittling name given to the small group of white Southerners who supported Reconstruction.

TEN YEARS AFTER the secession of South Carolina and less than six after the close of the consequent Civil War between the States, I became a South Carolina "carpetbagger." That is, I migrated from our "Empire" to our "Palmetto" State [New York to South Carolina]. Five years before, I had migrated from New Jersey, my native state, to New York; twenty-five years after that from New York to Ohio, and two years later from Ohio to Illinois—all without being called a "carpetbagger." But I was called a "carpetbagger" in South Carolina when in 1870 I migrated to that State from New York. . . .

All immigrants to South Carolina from our Northern States in the late 1860's and the early 1870's were called "carpetbaggers," if while there they got a living—more or less of it, and whether by honest earnings or dishonest graft—in connection with the public service. Those also who got their living in private employment, but who associated with the office-holding class, were called "carpetbaggers"; and those who pursued unofficial callings and had few official

graft
the acquiring of money by illegal or unfair means

associates or none became "carpetbaggers" upon going into politics. This if they were from any of our Northern States. If natives of South Carolina, they became "scalawags," regardless of any previous condition of honor or respectability.

—*From Louis F. Post,* Journal of Negro History. *In James P. Shenton, editor,* The Reconstruction: A Documentary History, 1865–1877. *G. P. Putnam's Sons, 1963.*

THINK ABOUT THIS

1. According to the writer, what types of people were called carpetbaggers and scalawags?
2. How do you think the writer felt about being called a carpetbagger?

Thomas Nast Draws a Carpetbagger

Opponents of Reconstruction were right about one thing: government corruption did become increasingly widespread in the years following the Civil War. However, politicians who used their political power for personal gain could be found just about everywhere—in the North and South, Republican and Democratic parties, federal and local governments. In this 1872 drawing, the famous political cartoonist Thomas Nast pictured Republican senator Carl Schurz as a corrupt carpetbagger. Schurz was a German immigrant who had settled in the northern United States and served as a major general in the Union army. After the war he moved south to Missouri, where he was elected to the U.S. Senate in 1869. A few years later, he joined a group of Republicans who broke away from the party, accusing President Grant of corruption and opposing his reelection. Nast was a dedicated supporter of the president, and he blasted

Schurz for his "betrayal." The caption he wrote for the cartoon read, "The bag in front of him, filled with others' faults, he always sees. The one behind him, filled with his own faults, he never sees."

1. How does Nast's drawing ridicule Schurz?
2. How does his caption help convey the cartoon's message?

Booker T. Washington Gets an Education

Before the Civil War few Southerners, white or black, had access to a free education. During Reconstruction, state governments established public school systems throughout the South, replacing and

A literature class at Hampton Normal and Agricultural Institute in 1899. Booker T. Washington attended the school from 1872 to 1875.

expanding the network of freedmen's schools. Charitable organizations also founded colleges and trade schools to offer black men and women the chance for higher learning. In his autobiography, *Up from Slavery,* Booker T. Washington described the challenges and excitement of getting an education. Born into slavery and freed at age seven by the Emancipation Proclamation, Washington had attended one of the South's first public schools for black children. He completed his education at the Hampton Normal and Agricultural Institute (now Hampton University) in Virginia and went on to become a famous public speaker, educator, and the founder of Tuskegee Institute in Alabama.

ONE DAY, WHILE AT WORK in the coal-mine, I happened to overhear two miners talking about a great school for coloured people somewhere in Virginia. This was the first time I had ever heard anything about any kind of school or college that was more pretentious than the little coloured school in our town. . . .

pretentious
ambitious

As they went on describing the school, it seemed to me that it must be the greatest place on earth, and not even Heaven presented more attractions for me at that time than did the Hampton Normal and Agricultural Institute in Virginia, about which these men were talking. I resolved at once to go to that school, although I had no idea where it was, or how many miles away, or how I was going to reach it. . . .

". . . not even Heaven presented more attractions for me at that time than did the Hampton Normal and Agricultural Institute."

I reached Hampton, with a surplus of exactly fifty cents with which to begin my education. To me it had been a long, eventful journey; but the first sight of the large, three-story, brick school building seemed to have rewarded me for all that I had undergone in order to reach the place. . . . It seemed to me to be the largest and most beautiful building I had ever seen. The sight of it seemed to give me new life. I felt that a new kind of existence had now begun—that life would now have a new meaning. I felt that I had reached the promised land, and I resolved to let no obstacle prevent me from putting forth the highest effort to fit myself to accomplish the most good in the world. . . .

I was among the youngest of the students who were in Hampton at that time. Most of the students were men and women—some as old as forty years of age. As I now recall the scene of my first year, I do not believe that one often has the opportunity of coming into contact with three or four hundred men and women who were so tremendously in earnest as these men and women were. Every hour was occupied in study or work. Nearly all had had enough actual contact with the world to teach them the need of education. Many of the older ones were, of course, too old to master the text-books very thoroughly, and it was often sad to watch their struggles; but they made up in earnestness much of what they lacked in books. Many of them were as poor as I was, and, besides having to wrestle with their books, they had to struggle with a poverty which prevented their having the necessities of life.

—*From Booker T. Washington,* Up From Slavery: An Autobiography. *New York: Doubleday, 1963.*

THINK ABOUT THIS

1. What did the opportunity to go to college mean to Washington?

2. What challenges did the freed slaves face in getting an education?

The Civil Rights Act of 1875 Prohibits Discrimination

Slavery was dead, but racial prejudice and discrimination were still very much alive. In 1870 Senator Charles Sumner introduced a second Civil Rights Bill to combat what he called "the last lingering taint [stain] of slavery." Sumner's bill prohibited discrimination in schools, juries, public transportation, and public facilities such as restaurants and theaters. White Southerners argued that the

Senator Charles Sumner in his study in 1871. Sumner believed that the federal government needed to do more to guarantee the rights of African Americans.

proposed legislation was unconstitutional because it was aimed at regulating private businesses and individuals. Many lawmakers also feared that the measure would destroy the South's new system of public schools, which, although they were segregated, did provide free education to all. These lawmakers were concerned that whites would refuse to allow their children to attend school side by side with black children. Despite these doubts the Senate approved the Civil Rights Bill in 1874, and the House passed it a year later—after removing the provision relating to schools.

BE IT ENACTED, That all persons within the jurisdiction of the United States shall be entitled to the full and equal enjoyment of the accommodations, advantages, facilities, and privileges of inns, public conveyances on land or water, theaters, and other places of public amusement; subject only to the conditions and limitations established by law, and applicable alike to citizens of every race and color, regardless of any previous condition of servitude.

". . . no citizen . . . shall be disqualified for service as juror . . . on account of race, color, or previous condition of servitude."

SECTION 2. That any person who shall violate the foregoing section by denying to any citizen . . . the enjoyment of any of the accommodations, advantages, facilities, or privileges . . . shall, for every such offense, forfeit and pay the sum of five hundred dollars to the person aggrieved thereby. . . .

SECTION 4. That no citizen possessing all other qualifications which are or may be prescribed by law shall be disqualified for service as juror in any court of the United States, or of any State, on account of race, color, or previous condition of servitude.

—*From the Civil Rights Act of 1875.* United States Statutes at Large, volume 18, p. 335, March 1, 1875.

THINK ABOUT THIS

1. What protections does the act extend to black citizens?

2. How would you answer arguments that Congress should not pass laws regulating private businesses and individuals?

John R. Lynch Denounces Segregation

The Civil Rights Act of 1875 had little effect on racial discrimination. Most public facilities in the South continued to discriminate against blacks, either by denying them service or confining them to separate, segregated areas. In the following address to Congress, Representative John R. Lynch described the segregation he encountered on his official trips to Washington, DC. Born into slavery, Lynch had been elected as U.S. representative from Mississippi in 1873.

THINK OF IT FOR A MOMENT; here am I, a member of your honorable body, representing one of the largest and wealthiest districts in the State of Mississippi, and possibly in the South; a district composed of persons of different races, religions, and nationalities; and yet, when I leave my home to come to the capital of the nation to take part in the deliberations of the House and to participate with you in making laws for the government of this great Republic, . . . I am treated, not as an American citizen, but as a brute. Forced to occupy a filthy smoking-car both night and day, with drunkards, gamblers, and criminals; and for what? Not that I am unable or unwilling to pay my way; not that I am obnoxious in my personal appearance or disrespectful in my conduct; but simply because I happen to be of a darker complexion. If this treatment was confined to persons of our own sex we could possibly afford to endure it. But such is not the case. Our wives and our daughters, our sisters and our mothers, are subjected to the same insults and to the same uncivilized treatment. . . . The only moments of my life when I am necessarily compelled to question my loyalty to my Government or my devotion to the flag of my country is when I read of outrages having been committed upon innocent colored people . . . , and when I leave my home to go traveling.

Mr. Speaker, if this unjust discrimination is to be longer tolerated by the American people, which I do not, cannot, and will not believe until I am forced to do so, then I can only say with sorrow

> *"I am treated, not as an American citizen, but as a brute . . . simply because I happen to be of a darker complexion."*

and regret that our boasted civilization is a fraud; our republican institutions a failure; our social system a disgrace; and our religion a complete hypocrisy.

—From John R. Lynch, speech to Congress, February 3, 1875.
In William L. Katz, Eyewitness: The Negro in American History.
New York: Pitman Publishing, 1968. Also available online at
http://www.law.nyu.edu/davisp/neglectedvoices/LynchFeb031875.html

THINK ABOUT THIS

1. How was Lynch discriminated against on his trips to Washington?

2. Are his arguments against discrimination based on facts, emotions, or a combination of both?

Chapter 5

The End of Reconstruction

MOST WHITE SOUTHERNERS bitterly opposed Reconstruction. They were still angry and humiliated over the loss of the Civil War, and they resented the continued presence of Northern troops and Freedmen's Bureau officials in the South. They also objected to the high taxes they were forced to pay to fund all the Reconstruction programs.

Over time Reconstruction opponents united in their efforts to overthrow the new Southern state governments. Calling for an end to Northern "oppression," they pressured the scalawags (white supporters of Reconstruction) to return to the "white man's party." In states with a large white population, that was often enough to vote the Republicans out of office. Elsewhere, terrorist groups such as the Ku Klux Klan used intimidation and violence to force freedmen and white Republicans to vote for the Democrats, or not vote at all.

By the late 1870s, Democrats had regained control of all Southern state governments. Reconstruction officially came to an end in 1877, when America's newly elected president, Rutherford B.

The end of Reconstruction began a long period of suffering for African Americans, who would not make real progress in gaining their civil rights for nearly a hundred years. This photograph of a thirteen-year-old sharecropper was taken in Georgia in 1937 by famed photojournalist Dorothea Lange.

Hayes, withdrew the last federal troops from the South. Over the next few years, Southern legislatures would pass laws depriving blacks of their civil rights and enforcing a rigid segregation of the races.

The "Good Old Rebel": An Anti-Reconstruction Song

The song "Good Old Rebel" was popular in the South long after the end of the Civil War. It is believed that the lyrics were written by Innes Randolph, a former Confederate officer. They expressed commonly held attitudes toward emancipation and the Reconstruction process.

O, I'm a good old Rebel,
Now that's just what I am,
For this "Fair Land of Freedom"
I do not give a damn!
I'm glad I fit [fought] against it,
I only wish we'd won,
And I don't want no pardon
For anything I've done.

I hates the Constitution,
This "Great Republic," too!
I hates the Freedman's Bureau
In uniforms of blue!
I hates the nasty eagle,
With all his brags and fuss,

"I hates the Constitution, This 'Great Republic,' too!"

And the lying, thieving Yankees,
I hates 'em wuss and wuss [worse and worse].

—From "O, I'm a Good Old Rebel." Available online at
http://www.nps.gov/pete/mahan/teachingtoolssongs.html and
http://home.earthlink.net/~poetry61-65/confederate/songs/rebel.html

THINK ABOUT THIS

Many Southerners continued to fight the Civil War long after
it was over, in some cases for decades. Was there any advantage to
this kind of thinking, or would they have benefited from letting their
anger go?

A Grand Jury Reports on the Ku Klux Klan

In the late 1860s resistance to Radical Reconstruction became
increasingly violent. White supremacists formed secret societies to
combat the political power of the freedmen and their supporters.
The largest and most brutal of these organizations was the "Invisi-
ble Empire of the South," commonly known as the Ku Klux Klan.
Organized around 1866 by Confederate veterans in Tennessee, the
group used intimidation and violence to keep blacks and white
Republicans from voting. Klan members wore ghostly white robes
and hoods to disguise their identities and frighten the superstitious.
They whipped, tortured, or murdered thousands of people and
burned homes, schoolhouses, and churches. In 1871 President
Grant appointed a federal grand jury to investigate Ku Klux Klan
activities. The jury's report included this copy of the loyalty oath

Klansmen, like those in this 1868 illustration, terrorized African Americans and kept many from voting and exercising other civil rights. The violence was so severe that in 1871 Congress authorized the president to use federal troops against the Klan.

taken by new Klan members. The report also recommended that the president use "the strong arm of the government" to suppress the Klan and similar terrorist groups.

I, _____, before the immaculate Judge of Heaven and earth, and upon the Holy Evangelists of Almighty God, do, of my own free will and accord, subscribe to the following sacredly binding obligation:

1. We are on the side of justice, humanity, and constitutional liberty, as bequeathed to us in its purity by our forefathers.

2. We oppose and reject the principles of the Radical Party.

3. We pledge mutual aid to each other in sickness, distress, and pecuniary embarrassment.

4. Female friends, widows, and their households shall ever be special objects of our regard and protection.

5. Any member divulging, or causing to be divulged, any of the foregoing obligations, shall meet the fearful penalty and traitor's doom, which is Death! Death! Death!

—From "Report of the Federal Grand Jury to the Judges of the U.S. Circuit Court, Columbia, S.C.," 42nd Congress, 2nd session, 1872. In Brenda Stalcup, editor, Reconstruction: Opposing Viewpoints. *San Diego, CA: Greenhaven Press, 1995.*

THINK ABOUT THIS

1. What do you think is meant by the word *purity* in section one?

2. Why do you think Southern government leaders were reluctant to take action against the Ku Klux Klan?

Mississippi Democrats Steal an Election

When intimidation and violence failed to keep blacks and white Republicans from voting, white supremacists often found ways to rig election results. D. J. Foreman was a black Republican leader from a small district in Mississippi that had an overwhelming majority of Republican voters. In testimony before a Senate committee investigating voting fraud, he explained how the Democrats had succeeded in "winning" a local election in 1875.

QUESTION: What did you propose to do at the election?

ANSWER: Some said not to go to the polls; some said they would go; some said they were afraid to go, and some said they were not, and they would go [even] if they got killed. . . .

QUESTION: Are your people armed generally? . . .

ANSWER: No, sir; they are poorly armed. . . .

QUESTION: When did you first know what the result was [in the election]?

ANSWER: I met Bazelius, clerk of the election, the next morning . . . , and I asked him what was the result of the election. He told me: "We beat you badly yesterday." I says, "No, you didn't; you polled forty-seven votes." He says, "It was you polled forty-seven votes, and we polled three hundred. You all voted democratic votes." . . .

QUESTION: Do you know anything more about what took place at the election?

ANSWER: [The whites] met the colored people, and would not allow them to come with arms; and the white people kept on theirs, and that scared the colored people. . . .

QUESTION: And the democrats carried their arms?

ANSWER: Yes, sir; and [they] told me that I would have to shut my mouth.

—From "Mississippi in 1875," Senate Report 527, Part II, 44th Congress, 1st Session. In William Loren Katz, Eyewitness: The Negro in American History. New York: Pitman Publishing, 1968.

THINK ABOUT THIS

1. What methods did the Democrats use to steal the election?

2. What steps could the federal government have taken to prevent this case of voting fraud?

Rutherford B. Hayes Approves the Compromise of 1877

By 1876, Democrats had overthrown, or "redeemed," the Reconstruction governments of all but three Southern states: South Carolina, Florida, and Louisiana. That year's presidential election pitted Rutherford B. Hayes, a moderate Republican, against Democratic candidate Samuel J. Tilden. In the three "unredeemed" states, both sides tried to influence the election's outcome through a variety of illegal means, from bribery to voter intimidation to miscounting. In the end, each of the states turned in two different sets of returns, one giving the victory to Hayes and the other to Tilden. To resolve the dispute, Congress appointed a special electoral commission, which included members from both parties. The commission worked

Rutherford B. Hayes had fought for the Union in the Civil War; his wife, Lucy, had been an abolitionist and was the first First Lady with a college degree. By the end of Hayes's second month as president, all federal forces had left Southern soil.

out a compromise that gave the presidency to Hayes, in return for his agreement to withdraw the federal troops from the South. In his inaugural address President Hayes expressed the hope that whites and blacks would work together to peacefully complete the process of Reconstruction.

THE EVILS WHICH AFFLICT the Southern States can only be removed or remedied by the united and harmonious efforts of both races, actuated by motives of mutual sympathy and regard; and while in duty bound and fully determined to protect the rights of all by every constitutional means at the disposal of my Administration, I am sincerely anxious to use every legitimate influence in favor of honest and efficient local *self*-government as the true resource of those States for the promotion of the contentment and prosperity of their citizens. In the effort I shall make to accomplish this purpose I ask the cordial cooperation of all who cherish an interest in the welfare of the country, trusting that party ties and the prejudice of race will be freely surrendered in behalf of the great purpose to be accomplished. . . .

At the basis of all prosperity, for [the South] as well as for every other part of the country, lies the improvement of the intellectual and moral condition of the people. Universal suffrage should rest upon universal education. To this end, liberal and permanent provision should be made for the support of free schools by the State governments, and, if need be, supplemented by legitimate aid from national authority.

"Let me assure my countrymen of the Southern States that it is my earnest desire to regard and promote their truest interest."

Let me assure my countrymen of the Southern States that it is my earnest desire to regard and promote their truest interest—

the interests of the white and of the colored people both and equally—and to put forth my best efforts in behalf of a civil policy which will forever wipe out in our political affairs the color line and the distinction between North and South, to the end that we may have not merely a united North or a united South, but a united country.

—*From Rutherford B. Hayes, Inaugural Address, March 5, 1877.*
Available online at http://www.bartleby.com/124/pres35.html

THINK ABOUT THIS

1. Why does Hayes believe that the races will be able to work together to restore the South?

2. Do you think that his hopes were realistic?

The Supreme Court Overturns the Civil Rights Act of 1875

With the overthrow of Republican governments and the withdrawal of federal troops, white rule was restored in the South. New all-white governments rolled back the advances of Reconstruction, reducing funds for black schools and imposing conditions that made it nearly impossible for African Americans to vote. Discriminatory laws gradually provided for the strict segregation of the races. In several key decisions the Supreme Court upheld these laws and ruled that measures designed to protect the rights of blacks were unconstitutional. In 1883 the Court struck down the Civil Rights Act of 1875, ruling that the federal government did not have the right to legislate against discrimination by private businesses and individuals. Speaking at a protest meeting in Washington, DC, Frederick Douglass blasted the decision.

THIS DECISION HAS INFLICTED a heavy calamity upon the seven millions of the colored people of this country, and left them naked and defenceless against the action of a malignant, vulgar and pitiless prejudice.

It presents the United States before the world as a nation utterly destitute of power to protect the rights of its own citizens. It can claim service and allegiance, loyalty and life of them, but it cannot protect them against the most palpable violation of [their] rights. . . .

In the name of common sense, I ask, what right have we to call ourselves a nation in view of this decision and this destitution of power?

In humiliating the colored people of this country, this decision humbles the nation.

> *"In humiliating the colored people of this country, this decision humbles the nation."*

—From a speech by Frederick Douglass, October 1883. In Henry McNeal Turner, The Barbarous Decision of the United States Supreme Court Declaring the Civil Rights Act Unconstitutional, 1883. *Available online at http://docsouth.unc.edu/church/turnerbd/turner.html*

THINK ABOUT THIS

1. What does Douglass say will be the result of the Supreme Court decision?
2. Why does he believe that the ruling hurts not only African Americans but the entire nation?

Black Sharecroppers Work Like Slaves

One of the most significant failures of Reconstruction was in the area of land reform. Radicals had advocated breaking up the old plantations and distributing the land to the freed slaves. However, supporters of land confiscation were unable to overcome fierce opposition from white Southerners and Northern moderates and conservatives. In the years following the Civil War, many landless freedmen ended up working as sharecroppers

A family of sharecroppers outside their house in Virginia. Reconstruction had failed most African Americans, who continued to live in poverty, to work like slaves, to face violence and prejudice, and to have no voice in American politics.

on white-owned farms, earning meager wages or a small portion of the harvest in return for their labor. In 1875 a congressional committee investigating working conditions in Louisiana heard this testimony from three black farmworkers, illustrating the inequities of the sharecropping system.

WE WORKED, OR MADE CONTRACT TO WORK, . . . on Mr. McMoring's place, and worked for one-third of the crop, and he was to find us all of our provisions; and in July, 1875, we was working alone in the field, and Mr. McMoring and McBounton came to us and says, "Well, boys, you all got to get away from here"; and . . . the two white men went and got sticks and guns, and told us that we must leave the place; and we told them that we would not leave it, because we don't want to give up our

". . . the two white men went and got sticks and guns, and told us that we must leave the place."

crop for nothing; and they told us that we had better leave, or we would not get anything; and we wanted justice, but [they] would not let us have justice. . . . They beat Isaiah Fuller, and whipped him, and then we got afraid, and we left the place; and we [have] about thirty acres in cotton, and the best cotton crop in that part of the parish; and we have about twenty-nine acres of corn, and about the best corn in the parish, and it is ripe, and the fodder ready to pull, and our cotton laid by; and [they] runned us off the place, and told us not to come back any more; and we were due [from] Mr. McMoring the sum of one hundred and eighty dollars and they told us that if they ever heard of it any more that they would fix us; and all the time that we were living and working on the place they would not half feed us; and we had to pay for all, or half of our rashings [rations], . . . and we worked for them as though we were slaves, and then [were] treated like dogs.

—From *Executive Document No. 30, 44th Congress, 2nd Session.* In Milton Meltzer, *The Black Americans: A History in Their Own Words.* New York: HarperCollins, 1984.

THINK ABOUT THIS

1. One land reform advocate argued that emancipating the slaves without giving them the land they needed to achieve economic independence was "only the mockery of freedom." How does this document illustrate that point?

2. How were the sharecroppers' working conditions different from their lives under slavery? How were they the same?

Time Line

APRIL 9, 1866

Congress passes the Civil Rights Act over President Johnson's veto.

JULY 16, 1866

Congress passes the Freedmen's Bureau Bill, extending the agency for one year.

MARCH 3, 1865

The Freedmen's Bureau is established.

APRIL 9, 1865

Confederate general Robert E. Lee surrenders to Union general Ulysses S. Grant, ending the Civil War.

JULY 24, 1866

Tennessee becomes the first Southern state to be readmitted to the Union.

Congress passes the Fourteenth Amendment.

JUNE 13, 1866

The Thirteenth Amendment is ratified, abolishing slavery throughout the United States.

DECEMBER 18, 1865

President Lincoln is assassinated, and Andrew Johnson is sworn in as president.

APRIL 14–15, 1865

Abraham Lincoln is sworn into office for a second term.

MARCH 4, 1865

Congress passes the First Reconstruction Act.

MARCH 2, 1867

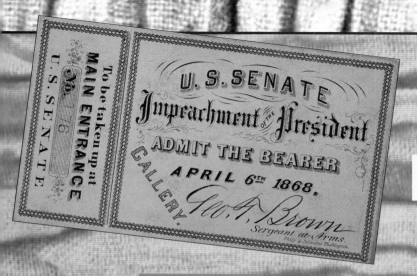

FEBRUARY 26, 1869

Congress passes the Fifteenth Amendment.

MAY 16, 1868

The Senate fails to convict Johnson.

The Fourteenth Amendment is ratified.

JULY 28, 1868

The House of Representatives votes to impeach President Johnson.

FEBRUARY 24, 1868

FEBRUARY 28, 1871

Congress passes the second Enforcement Act, combating fraud in voter registration.

FEBRUARY 3, 1870

The Fifteenth Amendment is ratified.

APRIL 20, 1871

Congress passes the third Enforcement Act, also known as the Ku Klux Klan Act, combating white supremacist groups.

MAY 31, 1870

Congress passes the first Enforcement Act, protecting the right to vote.

JUNE 10, 1872

The Freedmen's Bureau expires.

Georgia becomes the last Southern state to be readmitted to the Union.

JULY 15, 1870

SURRAT.   BOOTH.   HAROLD.

War Department, Washington, April 20, 1865.

$100,000 REWARD!

THE MURDERER

Of our late beloved President, Abraham Lincoln,

IS STILL AT LARGE.

$50,000 REWARD

Will be paid by this Department for his apprehension, in addition to any reward offered by Municipal Authorities or State Executives.

$25,000 REWARD

Will be paid for the apprehension of JOHN H. SURRAT, one of Booth's Accomplices.

$25,000 REWARD

Will be paid for the apprehension of David C. Harold, another of Booth's accomplices.

EDWIN M. STANTON, Secretary of War.

Grant is elected to a second term as president.

NOVEMBER 5, 1872

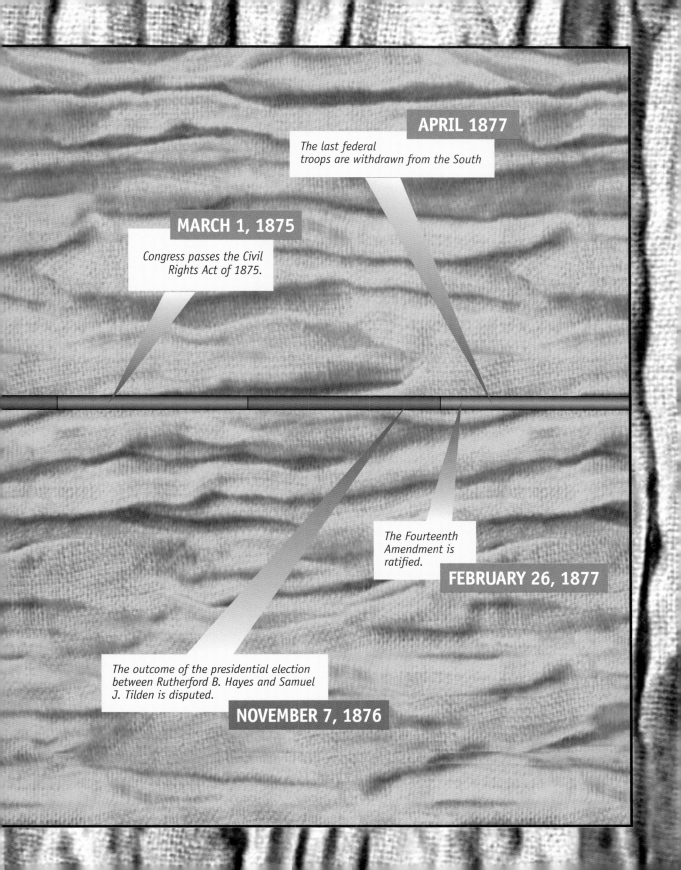

APRIL 1877

The last federal troops are withdrawn from the South

MARCH 1, 1875

Congress passes the Civil Rights Act of 1875.

The Fourteenth Amendment is ratified.

FEBRUARY 26, 1877

The outcome of the presidential election between Rutherford B. Hayes and Samuel J. Tilden is disputed.

NOVEMBER 7, 1876

A Thomas Nast cartoon depicting President Ulysses S. Grant

Glossary

abolitionists people who were in favor of abolishing, or putting an end to, slavery

Bushwhackers Confederates who fought as guerrillas during the Civil War, hiding out in the wild and ambushing Union troops. Some Bushwhackers continued their activities after the war's end, attacking freed slaves and their supporters.

charge a person who is entrusted to the care of another

commissary a store or an office where food and other supplies are distributed

confiscated seized by the government

enfranchisement the act of giving someone the right to vote

French Creoles persons of mixed French and black descent who live in and around Louisiana and often speak a simplified form of French called Creole. Creoles may also be whites of Spanish or French descent.

impeachment the act of charging a public official with crimes, in order to remove the official from office

naturalized admitted to citizenship

reprieves temporary delays of punishment

secede to formally withdraw from a group or an organization

suffrage the right to vote

To Find Out More

BOOKS

Beller, Susan Provost. *American Voices from the Civil War.* New York: Benchmark Books, 2003.

George, Charles. *Life under the Jim Crow Laws.* The Way People Live series. San Diego, CA: Lucent Books, 2000.

Golay, Michael. *Reconstruction and Reaction: The Emancipation of Slaves, 1861–1913.* New York: Facts on File, 1996.

Hakim, Joy. *Reconstruction and Reform.* A History of US series. New York: Oxford University Press, 1994.

Kallen, Stuart. *The Civil War and Reconstruction.* Edina, MN: Abdo Publishing, 2001.

Meltzer, Milton. *The Black Americans: A History in Their Own Words.* New York: HarperCollins, 1984.

Mettger, Zak. *Reconstruction: America after the Civil War.* New York: Lodestar Books, 1994.

Schomp, Virginia. *The Civil War.* Letters from the Battlefront series. New York: Benchmark Books, 2004.

———. *The Civil War.* Letters from the Homefront series. New York: Benchmark Books, 2002.

Stalcup, Brenda, ed. *Reconstruction.* Opposing Viewpoints series. San Diego: Greenhaven Press, 1995.

Wade, Linda R. *Reconstruction: The Years Following the Civil War.* Edina, MN: Abdo Publishing, 1998.

WEB SITES

The Web sites listed here were in existence in 2005, when this book was being written. Names or addresses may have changed since then.

In general, you will need to use caution when using the Internet to do research on a history topic. You will find numerous Web sites that look very attractive and professional. However, you should review these with a critical eye. Many Web sites, even the best ones, contain errors. Some acknowledge that fact by inserting disclaimers, or warnings that mistakes may have made their way into the site. In the case of primary sources, the creators of Web sites often transcribe previously published material, good or bad, accurate or inaccurate. A good rule to follow as you do research is to compare what you find in Web sites to the information in several other sources, such as librarian- or teacher-recommended reference works and major works of scholarship. When you do this, you will discover the many different versions of history.

America's Story from America's Library: Reconstruction (1866–1877)

http://www.americaslibrary.gov/cgi-bin/page.cgi/jb/recon

The Library of Congress presents this brief history of Reconstruction, which includes links to dozens of interesting stories about the people and events of the period.

Civil War Resources on the Internet: Abolitionism to Reconstruction (1830's–1890's)

**http://www.libraries.rutgers.edu/rul/rr_gateway/research_guides/
history/civwar.shtml**

This Rutgers University resource provides links to dozens of sites containing primary sources on the Civil War and Reconstruction.

Famous American Trials: The Andrew Johnson Impeachment Trial, 1868

**http://www.law.umkc.edu/faculty/projects/ftrials/impeach/
impeachmt.htm**

Created by a professor at the University of Missouri-Kansas Law School, this excellent Web site offers lots of information on the impeachment trial of Andrew Johnson, including a time line, photographs, drawings, and newspaper accounts.

Freedmen's Bureau Online

http://www.freedmensbureau.com

This site offers hundreds of Freedmen's Bureau records relating to labor, marriage, race riots, legal disputes, and murders and other crimes against freedmen.

Harp Week

http://www.harpweek.com

Explore nineteenth-century American history through news articles, editorials, illustrations, and cartoons from *Harper's Weekly* magazine.

Songs of the Civil War

http://www.nps.gov/pete/mahan/teachingtoolssongs.html

This National Park Service Web site offers words and sheet music for several Union and Confederate songs.

Index

Page numbers for illustrations are in boldface

ABOUT THE AUTHOR

Adriane Ruggiero has written numerous books about history, both ancient and modern, and international affairs. Her most recent publications for Marshall Cavendish Benchmark include a title in the Cultures of the Past series, *The Ottoman Empire,* and three other titles in the American Voices series: *World War I, The Great Depression,* and *World War II.* Ms. Ruggiero is also a frequent contributor to reference works such as *The Dictionary of the Middle Ages, The Encyclopedia of Ancient Greece and Rome,* and *Magill's Encyclopedia of Military History.*